Please return/renew this item by the last date shown.
Items may also be renewed by the internet*

https://library.eastriding.gov.uk

* Please note a PIN will be required to access this service
- this can be obtained from your library

LIVING ON AN ISLAND

Olivia is living as a self-imposed exile on a small island as she tries to recover from a broken heart. Her concerned best friend Abby insists on hiring a housekeeper to look after her whilst she paints — the handsome Kelly Miller, a trained army chef.

Kelly proves to be the perfect house-keeper, and also a dab hand at repairs, setting about fixing up the dilapi-dated house Olivia has dreams of one day turning into an artists' retreat. But Kelly has his own dreams — and when it looks like they may become reality, Olivia must decide whether to risk her heart again . . .

SARAH PURDUE

LIVING ON AN ISLAND

Complete and Unabridged

LINFORD
Leicester

First published in Great Britain in 2020 by
D.C. Thomson & Co. Ltd.
Dundee

First Linford Edition
published 2023
by arrangement with
the author and
D.C. Thomson & Co. Ltd.
Dundee

A catalogue record for this book is available
from the British Library.

ISBN 978–1–4448–5144–1

Perfect Stranger

'It's non-negotiable, Liv,' Abby said, her voice carrying down the crackling phone line.

Olivia sighed. She knew her friend meant well but this really did feel like a step too far.

'I understand why you want to be there.' Abby paused briefly and obviously decided that now was not the time to rake up the painful past. 'But if you are going to live on an island in the middle of nowhere, you need someone to take care of you.'

'I can take care of myself. I'm not a child,' Olivia said, knowing that she sounded exactly like a child, even to her own ears, 'and besides, I have Mabel.' She leaned down and rubbed the ears of her miniature sausage dog.

'Liv, the last time I visited you hadn't eaten for days and no, black coffee does not count. And you know I love Mabel but she doesn't talk or make you dinner.'

1

'I get lost in my work; you should at least understand that.'

'Of course I do, you're an artist and can't be troubled by earthly things. As your agent I understand, but as your friend I worry about you. You need to eat and you need someone to do all the basic household stuff so that you can concentrate on your work.'

'I don't want to be interrupted all the time,' Olivia protested, her mind conjuring up an older lady, like a kindly auntie, who would interrupt every ten minutes asking if she would like a nice cup of tea.

'You won't be. I have found the perfect person, I promise — and not only that, they will be arriving today.' Abby said it as if it were a done deal, which Olivia suspected at this point it was. 'It's either that or you move back to London.'

Olivia shuddered at the thought.

'No chance and besides, my work has been so much better since I've been here.'

'I won't argue with that but you do need someone to look after you and since

I have to run the gallery here that person has to be someone other than me.

'You need some companionship, Liv. It's not good for you to be there on your own. You've done that and now it's the time to let people back into your life.'

Olivia swallowed the lump in her throat.

'I have friends,' she managed to croak.

'You do, but you haven't been in touch with any of them for months.' Abby's voice was gentle but the pain was still real for Olivia.

'We all love you but we also know how difficult this is. I think maybe you need someone new, who wasn't part of your life back here. Someone who didn't know Ted.'

Hearing her fiancé's name out loud made Olivia gasp and she bit her lip to fight back the tears that were forming.

'Everyone was incredibly kind and supportive but after a few months they started to get back to their normal lives.' Olivia shook her head at the memory. It wasn't as if she blamed them, it was just that she couldn't do that.

'My world had stopped and I didn't know what to do. Ted and I were supposed to be getting married and then . . . then he was gone. I didn't even get a chance to say goodbye.' Olivia couldn't finish the sentence.

'I know, love. I know. And everyone understands but I think the time for isolation is over. You need to take some baby steps and you also need to be looked after, just for a bit.'

'Fine,' Olivia said, staring out of the large picture window that ran the length of her studio, 'but they'll have a game getting over here today in this weather.'

'I've spoken to Derek and he said it shouldn't be a problem.'

Olivia looked out at the stormy seas and the waves crashing on the beach. Derek was an experienced sailor and fisherman but she doubted that even he would want to brave the half a mile of so of sea that cut her tiny island off from the mainland.

'And if it is then I'm sure tomorrow

will be fine,' Abby said. 'Hopefully you will have some more pieces for me, too?'

Olivia turned from the view and studied her works in progress. There were lots of them but most of them were not finished.

'Maybe next week,' she said, almost to herself.

'Next week will be fine,' Abby said in the kind of voice that suggested it wasn't really but would have to do.

'And you know if you need a break you could always bring them yourself?' she added hopefully.

'I'll make sure I have a couple done for next week,' Olivia said, ignoring the suggestion.

There was no way she could go to London, not now, and she was starting to wonder if she could ever bring herself to visit there again. Too many memories, too much sadness associated with the place.

At least here on the Ingleside island there were no such memories. It was a fresh start and a place that she felt she could probably live for the rest of her life.

'OK, well let me know how it goes. I'm sure you'll be thanking me once you have a few home-cooked meals conjured up for you.'

'I'm sure I will,' Olivia said, now feeling a little guilty that she was giving her best friend such a hard time. 'Thank you.'

Abby laughed.

'You need this, Liv, just trust me. Now have you got a pen?'

'Why do I need a pen?' Olivia asked distractedly.

'Do you want to know details, like their name? It might be a bit awkward if you don't.'

Olivia rolled her eyes.

'I don't need a pen, just tell me.'

'Kelly Miller.'

Olivia considered this for a moment. Kelly sounded like a young person's name so maybe her concerns about a kindly but interfering auntie-figure were unfounded.

'And remember you may not think

you need this but you do, so let's give it a chance,' Abby said.

'I'll give you a call in a few days and let you know how we are doing.'

'You do that, and I'm here if you ever want to chat. Take care, Liv.'

'You, too,' Olivia said before hanging up. She looked out across the water once more. The mainland had almost completely disappeared in the downfall. There was no way Derek was coming over today so at least that gave her a day to psych herself up to having a house guest.

Mabel was starting to pace up and down and Olivia knew that meant it was time for a walk.

'I get the message,' Olivia said, smiling down at her. 'Time to go for a stroll?'

Mabel barked.

'It's still windy so we'll both need our coats but at least it's stopped raining.'

Mabel wriggled with excitement as Olivia slipped her doggy coat over her and then pulled on her own heavy waxed jacket. Abby might be right about the meals but Mabel was excellent company and Olivia never felt alone with her small dog by her side.

They stepped outside into the wind. It was late afternoon in spring, just after the clocks had gone forward, which meant stormy weather and the odd day of sunshine but Olivia didn't mind.

She always thought that London didn't really experience weather, not like here in the channel that ran along the south west coast. This was real weather and nature at its best. The island was less than a kilometre wide and so she and Mabel normally walked around it as their last leg stretch before turning in for the night.

Olivia patted her pocket.

'Right. I've got the torch in case you dawdle till the sun goes down. Let's go.'

Mabel didn't need a lead on the island, and gambled off. Olivia was always surprised at how fast such a small dog, with such little legs, could go. She followed Mabel down the path that led from the house to the beach and then they walked along the shore.

The small jetty was empty and there was no sign of Derek or his small boat. Not that she was surprised. The supplies weren't urgent and she suspected that her new housekeeper might baulk at setting sail in rough weather.

Mabel scampered on down the beach and then disappeared from view. Olivia wasn't worried since there was nowhere the dog could get lost and nothing on the island that could hurt her.

When the barking started Olivia assumed that Mabel was chasing seagulls, a hobby of the pup if Olivia had let her get away with it. But still she hurried to catch up. If she wasn't careful Mabel would like roll in some smelly seaweed and would then require a bath.

She rounded the next cove and stopped still. There was a small motorboat pulled up on to the shore and a figure standing beside it. Even from this distance, Olivia knew it wasn't Derek. Derek was a compact, well-muscled man but he was shorter than her, perhaps five foot five, and the stranger was much taller than that.

Olivia sighed. All the maps said that the island was private property but that didn't stop the odd day tripper trying their luck.

She hurried along the beach and could make out that the man, she could see that now, had Mabel in his arms and Mabel was licking his nose.

'I'm sorry — this island is private property. I'm going to have to ask you to leave.' Olivia glared at Mabel, who was now lying on her back in the man's arms and having her tummy tickled.

'It's all right,' the man said with a trace of an accent that Olivia couldn't identify, 'I'm supposed to be here.'

Olivia felt herself bristle a little. The cheek of this guy!

'I'm the owner of this island and I'm telling you that you aren't.' She felt her pocket, trying to see if she had her mobile phone with her. Not that she had much chance of a signal on this side of the island but the man didn't have to know that.

Before she could say anything else, the man had juggled Mabel into one arm and was holding out his hand to shake.

'Kelly Miller. I'm your new house-keeper.'

Olivia stared at the outstretched hand. There had to be some kind of mistake. She and Abby had never discussed the gender of her housekeeper but she had assumed that Abby would hire a woman.

'Kelly?' was the first word out of Olivia's mouth and she winced. No doubt Kelly had experienced a lot of comments about his first name all his life.

'After my mum. She died when I was born.'

'I'm so sorry . . .' she started to say.

'Because my dad called me a girl's name or because my mum died?'

Olivia looked up sharply but the man was smiling gently as if to tell her that it was OK and that he got that question a lot.

'Both?' Olivia said, before she realised what she was saying.

11

Now Kelly's smile broke in a broad grin.

'I like your honesty,' he said. 'My dad's actually American and Kelly is a fairly common boy's name over there. Of course being a boy named Kelly in the UK was more of a challenge.'

Olivia nodded as she tried to process all of the information.

'I'm afraid there has been some kind of mistake,' she said.

A housekeeper was one thing but a man? There was no way she was ready to have a man, a handsome man at that, on the island with her. What was Abby thinking?

Olivia frowned. She suspected she knew exactly what Abby was thinking. But Olivia knew she wasn't ready to let another person in to her life. What if something happened to them like it had to Ted? She couldn't bear the thought of it.

'I don't think so. I've been employed by Abby Bowerman as a housekeeper and cook. I trained as a chef in the army and I have a host of references if you are concerned.' It was then that Olivia noticed he was carrying a small rucksack, like the kind you would take out on a day's walking.

Olivia nodded but she was still sure there had been some kind of mistake.

'Did Abby know that you are . . .' Olivia couldn't finish the sentence, she was starting to feel foolish and make herself come across as a nun or something.

'I think when I met her, I may have given the game away.' Kelly smiled but it was gentle and understanding and Olivia wondered how much Abby had told him.

'Abby said that the place needed doing up and I've been working as a handyman so she seemed to think I was qualified.'

At that moment there was a rumble of thunder and the light levels dropped. They both looked up at the sky and Mabel whimpered. It was clear that it would not be safe for Kelly to get back in his motorboat and go back to the mainland.

'Let's head back to the house. We can sort things out there.'

'No problem,' Kelly said, keeping a tight hold of Mabel, who was now trying to hide inside his raincoat. He unzipped his coat and Mabel burrowed inside before Kelly zipped it up again.

'Cute dog,' Kelly said and Olivia nodded. Mabel was usually not great with strangers but she seemed to have gone all gooey over Kelly. Olivia led the way down the path and he followed her back up to the house.

'The roof could do with some attention,' he observed as they stepped into the hall. Olivia couldn't argue with that, since there were buckets and saucepans all over the house to collect the rainwater that leaked in.

'How about I make us a hot drink and pull something together for supper? I expect you'll be wanting to speak to Abby?'

Olivia wondered briefly if Kelly had the power to read her mind. It was an unsettling thought but he had guessed right.

She had been trying to think of a way to get rid of him so she could speak to Abby. Speak to Abby and demand to know exactly what she had been thinking.

'That would be great, thanks. The kitchen is through there.' Olivia pointed to the left.

'I'll find my way around, don't worry.' Kelly flashed her one more smile and Mabel trotted along beside him to the kitchen.

Olivia went right and turned into the small room that served as her office. She suspected that it had once been the housekeeper's sitting-room. The house was nearly 200 years old and owners from the past had brought full contingents of servants with them. The house was in a poor state now but had once been very grand and used as a sort of holiday home by generations of rich merchants and landed gentry.

Olivia picked up her mobile phone and wasn't surprised that she had no signal, even with the signal booster that

Abby had insisted was installed.

She turned to her computer. She would write an e-mail and send it. It wouldn't go until the signal was restored but hopefully, once the storm abated, it would disappear into the ether and she could get some kind of answer from her best friend.

The Trial Begins

Olivia dawdled in the office for as long as she could. She tried to pretend to herself that she was catching up on admin but in truth, with the WiFi and phone down, there was very little she could actually do.

She could hear the sounds of pots and pans being placed on the wood-burning stove and could only imagine what Kelly was pulling together from the pantry. It was full of tins, that again Abby had insisted that she have, but very little fresh food, since Derek hadn't been able to make his run.

Olivia's thoughts turned to how Kelly had arrived. He had said he was in the army but still it had been a slightly crazy plan to hire a motorboat in the current weather. She wondered if that was a clue to Kelly's personality but brushed it aside. She didn't need to be thinking about stuff like that.

At that moment the necklace around

her throat seemed to weigh heavy on her chest and she lifted a hand to grip the ring that hung there. The memories and sense of loss were never far away.

Olivia shook herself. There would be time to remember later. In order to survive she had built a sort of mental box to put all those thoughts and feelings in and she only allowed herself to open it when she was in bed at night. To begin with it had been so overwhelming that she hadn't been able to even get out of bed and so she had slowly, carefully built up the box so that she could function, so that she could paint.

It had been nearly a year and if asked she told people she was doing fine. In reality she was merely surviving but even that seemed like progress to her.

Right now she needed to focus on the stranger who was making her dinner and figure out a way to tell him politely that she wanted him to leave in the morning.

Walking down the short hall she could tell that Kelly was a good cook. She had no idea how he had managed to turn the tinned goods from the pantry into something that smelled so delicious but he had.

She peeked through the open door. The round wooden table was laid and Kelly was standing stirring a pot on the range. He must have heard her coming because he turned and smiled and despite her misgivings Olivia smiled back.

'Did you speak to Abby?' he asked before using a ladle to spoon out some sort of stew that was complete with dumplings,

'No — the phone and internet are down. I've sent her an e-mail but I suspect it won't go till the morning.'

Kelly nodded but said nothing and placed the two bowls on to the table.

Olivia took a seat and used a spoon to try the stew.

'Well?' Kelly asked before starting on his own bowl.

'Delicious. How did you manage it with just the tinned food?'

'The army mainly had tinned and

dried food so I'm used to it, but in truth it's all about the spices.'

Olivia could feel the meal warm her insides. It was a sensation that had been lacking in her life. The most she had really managed was some toast but it felt good to be eating proper food.

'I think I should start on the roof tomorrow; it seems the most urgent problem.'

Olivia nodded, wondering how to tell him that she wasn't sure she wanted him to stay. He must have caught her expression.

'I know you need to speak with Abby but I can probably patch the roof in a morning and then head back to the mainland, if that's what you decide.'

Olivia could feel some colour rise up her cheeks. He was being so reasonable it was embarrassing that she felt the way she did.

'I don't think that it's particularly fair to ask you to do that,' Olivia said, concentrating on her food and hoping that Kelly wouldn't notice her blushing.

'I don't mind. I'm not good at sitting about doing nothing.'

Olivia felt as though she should ask Kelly about himself. It seemed the polite thing to do but it was almost as if she had forgotten how to interact with another human being, particularly one that she didn't know.

Kelly ate and seemed unaffected by what Olivia perceived to be the uncomfortable silence and once more, she wondered exactly how much of her story Abby had told him.

When she had finished Kelly cleared the things away.

'I can do that,' Olivia said, feeling as if she should make some kind of contribution.

'This is what I'm here for,' Kelly said, 'even if it's only temporarily.'

Olivia sat in her chair and watched him stack the dishes beside the sink and run some hot water into the bowl. She was being selfish, she knew. Any decision she made didn't just affect her but Kelly, too. If she sent him away tomorrow then he would no doubt have to go back to looking for another job.

She shook her head. What if he had turned down other jobs to take this one? What if she let him go and he was unemployed for a while?

'Maybe we could do a two-week trial?' Olivia made herself say the words out loud before she could change her mind. 'You know — to see if you are happy and if I . . .' Olivia couldn't bring herself to say the word 'happy', it didn't seem possible.

'Sounds good,' Kelly said as he continued the washing up. 'Do you want a coffee?'

'I'll make it,' Olivia said, getting to her feet. It was nice to have someone to help out but she didn't want Kelly to feel like he was a slave or that she wasn't capable of looking after herself.

Kelly wiped his hands on the tea towel and accepted the mug of coffee.

'Thanks. I might go and get settled in. I expect you have painting to be getting on with.'

'Yes,' Olivia said although she hadn't actually planned to do any more that evening but she didn't think she could say so now. 'Your room is at the top of the stairs and turn left, last one down the corridor. I hope it's OK.'

'Thanks,' Kelly said, grabbing his small rucksack.

'Is that all you brought with you?'

'Army folk travel light,' Kelly said with a grin, 'but actually I left the rest of the luggage with Derek.'

Olivia nodded.

'I'm sure he'll bring it over tomorrow with the supplies.'

'I hope you don't mind but I added a few things to the list. I can cook dried and tin food but you can't beat a bit of fresh.'

'Of course,' Olivia said, wondering why she hadn't thought of that herself and it made her realise just how lost in her own head she had been.

'Well, goodnight,' Kelly said and strode out of the kitchen.

'Night,' Olivia called after him.

★ ★ ★

Olivia woke with a start. The sun was shining outside which told her that she had slept longer than was usual for her these days. She moved to the side of the bed. There was no sign of Mabel, who usually remained curled up beside her until Olivia got up.

She found her slippers and pulled on her dressing gown. Opening her bedroom door she could hear the sound of someone moving quietly around the kitchen. She would never say it out loud but it wasn't a bad feeling that there was someone else in the old house.

For so long she had felt the solitude was what she needed but there was something comforting to know that she wasn't completely alone. Kelly seemed to understand that her need for solitude and she felt sure he would find enough to do in the house to keep him busy. Maybe Abby was right after all, she mused.

In the kitchen, Kelly was preparing breakfast. There were eggs scrambling in the pan and the smell of toast.

'Morning,' he said, gesturing for her to take a seat. 'Breakfast is a little limited but I have asked Derek to bring some bacon and sausages, so tomorrow will be better.'

Kelly placed a plate in front of Olivia. There was toast, some tinned mushrooms and tomatoes and a pile of scrambled eggs. Olivia never usually bothered with breakfast, except for a black coffee and was about to say so but her rumbling stomach would have made a liar of her.

'Thanks.' She tucked in and Kelly started to clean up. 'Aren't you going to join me?'

'I've had mine,' Kelly said. 'I'm working on a list of things that need attention. Once I have my list I'll get started.'

Olivia nodded and smiled, trying to ignore the strange sensation inside her. Was she disappointed? She shook her head as if to clear it. There was no reason for them to take all their meals together. Olivia was fairly sure that was one of the things she had told Abby she wanted — to be left alone and not inter-rupted and not all of her reasons were to do with her painting.

'If you want coffee and biscuits then give me a shout. I've made some sandwiches for lunch so help yourself whenever you're ready.' Kelly wiped down the kitchen side. 'Just stack your plates when you're done and I'll wash up later.'

And then he was gone. It seemed likely that Abby had given very specific instructions and that Kelly was happy to follow them. She had to give Abby credit for that.

Thinking of Abby she took her plates to the sink and washed them up. She could do that at least. Once that was done, she carried her mug through to her office.

She turned on her mobile phone and was pleased to see that she had a signal. Abby had probably read her e-mail by now but Olivia thought it was quicker to speak to her friend and so dialled her number.

'I know what you are going to say. I've read your e-mail,' Abby said.

'And hello and good morning to you,' Olivia said with a smile. She couldn't blame her friend. Last night when she had written the e-mail she was determined that Kelly should leave as soon as possible and had made that abundantly clear.

'You sound ... OK? I know that Kelly may not have been what you were expecting . . .' Abby's voice trailed off, as if she had decided that the less she said the better.

'You could have told me! Talk about embarrassing! I practically ordered him off the island.'

'And yet he is still there?' Abby said somewhat mischievously.

Olivia sighed.

'I could hardly make him tackle the rough waters again, could I? Especially since you employed him.'

'OK, I admit that I could have told you but how is it going?'

'All right, actually.' And Olivia was a

little surprised at her own words.

'Kelly's won you over, then,' Abby said, a little too triumphantly for Olivia's liking.

'We've come to an agreement of a two-week trial,' Olivia said a little stiffly. She didn't want to be won over by anyone.

'What I meant was he seemed to understand that you needed your space,' Abby said carefully. 'I interviewed some women as well but I got the impression that they would smother you with kindness. And most of them wouldn't be able to fix the roof for you.'

'He has already sorted out a list of jobs so I'm sure he'll keep busy.'

'Which means you can get on and paint?' Abby said. It was more like a question than a statement.

'Yes, I can get on and paint and you can stop worrying about whether I'm eating enough.'

'He's a good cook, too. I got him to come round to mine and cook for me. I wanted to check that he was as good as his CV said he was.'

Olivia raised an eyebrow to herself.

'Did you now?' Olivia said teasingly.

'Nothing like that. Dan had to work and it seemed the best way to interview someone.'

'Uh huh,' Olivia said, smiling. 'And what did Dan say?'

'Well, he enjoyed the leftovers,' Abby said and they both giggled. Dan was so laid back he wouldn't have batted an eyelid at the idea of Abby having a hand-some guy round to cook her dinner.

Olivia blinked. It was the first time she had thought that about Kelly. It wasn't as if she hadn't noticed. He was well built and looked accustomed to working out-doors but what her brain hadn't allowed her to process was the fact that he had a warm smile that seemed to involve his whole face, chocolate brown eyes and a gentle way about him.

'Liv?'

'Sorry?' Olivia said, realising that she had not heard a word that Abby had said.

'I said, let me know how it goes. If Kelly doesn't work out I still think you need someone else over there with you. What if you had an accident or became ill and couldn't get to the phone?'

Olivia sighed. She and Abby had had this conversation many times and if nothing else Kelly's presence might negate the need for them to keeping talking over the same issue.

'I will and I'll get some new paintings over to you soon.'

'OK, honey, let me know if you need anything.'

'I will. Thanks, Abby.'

They hung up. Looking out of the window in the office Olivia could see Kelly run a ladder against the side of the house and swiftly climb it. She realised she was staring and so quickly hurried out of the room. If Kelly was staying out of the way so as not to distract her then the least she could do was get on with some painting.

No Strings Attached

When Olivia was painting, time seemed to stand still, in her studio at least. Mabel barked and that meant she could probably do with a leg stretch. One glance at the clock on her phone told Olivia it was nearly three in the afternoon and now she thought about it she was feeling hungry.

She pulled open the studio door and shuffled across to the kitchen. Just as promised there was a plate of ham sandwiches in the fridge. Olivia put the kettle on the stove and wondered if she should go and find Kelly and ask him if he wanted a cup of tea.

Mabel must have read her mind because she suddenly dashed out of the front door and so Olivia followed. Kelly was walking up the path from the beach, pulling the wooden trolley that Olivia used to bring supplies up from the jetty.

He raised a hand in greeting and Mabel threw herself at him. Kelly dropped the handle of the trolley just in time to catch the crazy pup.

Olivia hurried down towards Kelly and picked up the handle of the trolley.

'I'll do that,' Kelly said.

'I've been doing it ever since I arrived, I'm sure I can cope.' Olivia winced at her own tone. She didn't mean to sound so churlish. It was just that she was fed up with the assumption that she couldn't look after herself, even though she knew deep down that she hadn't been doing a particularly good job of it.

Kelly didn't look as if he had taken the words to heart and merely cradled Mabel like a baby in his arms. The trolley was heavier than Olivia remembered and one look told her there was a lot more food than she usually ordered, not to mention a large rucksack which was presumably the rest of Kelly's luggage.

'Derek has picked up the boat and taken it to the mainland. He says we are in for some more storms so I'm going to finish patching the roof before tea. It's just a temporary job. Once the weather is better I'll look at fixing it properly, although I will need some timber and supplies from the mainland.'

'Order what you need. I have a credit card that you can use for expenses.' Olivia wondered if that made her sound as if she were a millionaire. She was comfortably off but not in that league.

'I mean, within reason,' she added hastily. 'If it's a big expense then it's probably best we discuss it first.'

'Of course. It shouldn't be too bad. I need to replace a couple of cross beams and then it's just new tiles. A few hundred at most.'

Olivia nodded. She knew that to get an outside company in to do the work would more likely cost thousands and she made a mental note to check that Kelly was receiving a fair wage for all the work he was doing. As well as being her agent and best friend, Abby dealt with the money side of things and so was paying Kelly direct.

'I was planning to cook steak for dinner but that means I'll need to set a time.

Steak doesn't do so well if it's left sitting on the warming plate for too long.'

Olivia felt her mouth water and then her stomach joined in with a loud, appreciative rumble. Kelly chuckled.

'Can I take that as a yes?'

Olivia nodded, blushing a little.

'Well, let me know when you want to eat. I'll need about half an hour but I'm happy to eat whenever suits.'

'Thanks,' Olivia said. 'It depends a little where I'm at with my latest painting.'

'No problem, I'm used to eating early or late.'

They walked the rest of the way back to the house in companionable silence. Olivia wondered if this all really might work out.

Maybe Abby was right and it was time she had some company. Company on her own terms and that she could ask to leave her alone without feeling embarrassed.

She liked being on her own but even she had to admit that it had been lonely and not good for her state of mind. A no-strings-attached, professional working relationship could be just the thing.

'I'm going to start patching the roof. Just give me a shout if I'm disturbing you.'

'I'm sure it will be fine,' Olivia said, realising that she had been lost in thought and quite glad that Kelly couldn't read her mind. 'And besides, it needs doing.'

'Great. Shout when you want to eat.' Kelly said, taking the trolley handle from her and heading in the direction of the kitchen.

Mabel barked at her feet and danced around her. Olivia looked down.

'Sure, if you want to go and see what he's up to but don't get in the way. And no climbing any ladders.'

Mabel looked her and if it was possible the dog looked confused. Olivia laughed and gestured for Mabel to go. She watched the dog trot in the direction of the kitchen.

'Hello, you. Have you come to keep an eye on me?' Olivia heard Kelly's voice in the distance and then Mabel's bark which was clearly telling him that was exactly what she was intending to do. She heard Kelly's answering rumble of laughter and shook herself. She needed to get back to work, not stand around all day.

Kelly seemed determined not to distract her and it would be embarrassing if she gave in to being distracted by him. She popped back into the kitchen and helped herself to the plate of sandwiches before disappearing back into the studio.

★ ★ ★

Olivia wasn't sure what the time was but judging by the fading light it was getting late. She had daylight light-bulbs and so could work in her studio into the evening but it was not the same as working in real daylight. There was a scrabbling at the door and Olivia got up to let Mabel in.

'Have you had fun?' she asked, scooping the little dog up into her arms. Mabel licked her nose and she took that as an affirmative.

'What do you think?' Olivia said, turning Mabel so she could see her latest work in progress. It was a moody beach scene that she had sketched some weeks ago but she hadn't been happy with the painting itself. Today she had worked on lightening the sky and giving the effect of the sun breaking through after the storm and she was feeling quite pleased with it.

'Another day and I think I will have a few to send to Aunty Abby.'

There were sounds of someone moving around in the house and Mabel wriggled in her arms. She put the dog down and followed her.

'Hey, I hope I didn't disturb you,' Kelly said as he quietly rested a pan back on the stove.

'No, I was finishing up for the day,' Olivia said, taking in the signs of food preparations.

'I was just getting everything ready but I can start cooking if you're ready to eat.'

'Please,' Olivia said, thinking this was better than staying in a hotel.

'The roof is all patched up so we should be fine for the next storm. Once it's passed I'll head over to the mainland for a day to get what I need to make permanent repairs.'

'Sounds good,' Olivia said.

'There's beer in the fridge,' Kelly said, 'or wine, if you prefer.'

'Beer's good. Do you want one?' Olivia asked as she pulled the fridge open and took in the well laden shelves. She didn't think it had been so full in all the time she had been on the island.

'Please,' Kelly said. Olivia removed the bottle tops and handed one to Kelly before taking a seat. She had been thinking of going upstairs to have a bath but it seemed rude to leave Kelly to cook with no company. He had of course been working all day and fixing the roof was definitely harder work than painting all day.

'How's the painting going?' Kelly asked, looking up from the frying pan. 'I'm assuming I'm allowed to ask you that?'

'Today it's fine as it's going well but I can't guarantee that I will always respond positively.'

Kelly nodded and he looked as if he understood which surprised Olivia a little. Creativity was a funny thing. When it was flowing it was great but when it was a struggle it could feel like she would never be able to paint ever again. People who didn't paint rarely understood the struggle.

She felt she ought to ask Kelly something about himself. It was only polite, wasn't it? She wouldn't admit it out loud but she was also a little curious about the man. It seemed an unlikely job for anyone other than a sort of motherly figure.

'So how did you come to take the job?' Olivia asked in what she hoped sounded a casual kind of way.

'I left the army eighteen months ago and haven't really settled to anything. I've done a bit of handyman work and some chef work but you always have to work to a prescribed menu unless you are in charge and I found that a little frustrating. I saw this job advertised and it seemed kind of perfect.'

Olivia laughed.

'An island in the middle of nowhere is your idea of perfect?'

'I'm pretty self-sufficient and I have to admit that life in a city never really suited me.' He looked up from stirring a pan, his face slightly flushed with the heat from the stove. 'It shouldn't be that much of a surprise, should it? You seem to like it here.'

'Ah, but I'm an artist and everyone knows we are a little odd.' There was no way that Olivia was ready to share the real reasons she had exiled herself.

She looked up to see that Kelly had raised an eyebrow and she blushed as she realised what she had said.

'Not that I'm saying you're odd or anything . . .' She knew she was digging a hole but didn't seem to be able to stop herself. Thankfully Kelly stepped in before she could make matters more embarrassing.

'I've been called worse,' he said with

40

a smile. 'I wondered if you might want to keep this place a secret, you know, because you like it.'

'I do,' Olivia said slowly. 'It is very peaceful here and I like that.'

'There is definitely something special about this place,' Kelly said, turning his attention back to his cooking. Or was he avoiding making eye contact?

Olivia couldn't be sure but then immediately told herself off for making assumptions. She could only put it down to the fact she had had very little company over the last few months, aside from Mabel. Maybe she had lost her ability to read people?

'Do you mind me asking if you own it?' Kelly asked.

'I sort of inherited it,' she said, thinking that at least this was safer ground.

'How does anyone 'sort of' inherit anything?' Kelly asked, flashing her a curious look.

'Well, it was owned by a reclusive artist and he had no family. Or at least no family that he wanted to leave his studio to, so instead he ran a competition to find a painter to inherit it.'

'Wow!' Kelly said.

'I know,' Olivia said taking a sip of beer. 'I didn't even enter.'

'Then how did you win?' Kelly asked, expertly flipping over the steaks he had in the pan.

'Well, he wasn't happy with those who did enter and so he visited some small art galleries and saw my work.'

'And he left you the island?'

Olivia nodded. She still couldn't quite believe it herself. And it had been an absolute godsend after all that had happened. She had a place she could legitimately retreat to.

'I'd like eventually to turn it into an artists' retreat. I know that's what the artist wanted me to do and it seems only right to share it with other budding painters. But I need to fix the place up and spend some money on it — maybe build some more accommodation — but that will have to wait until I've sold some more work.'

'Well if you need a chef for your artists' retreat, I volunteer,' he said with a grin.

He turned back to his cooking and Olivia studied him. Would he really want to do that? It seemed a strange choice for him, to cut himself off from the rest of the world. Maybe he liked the peace and quiet like he had said. Or maybe there was more to it. One thing for sure, Olivia was curious about Kelly's story and she was determined to find out.

A Devastating Blow

'I've left some soup in the fridge and fresh bread on the side,' Kelly said as Olivia drank her cup of morning coffee. 'I'm sure I'll be back before low tide but I'll let you know if I get stuck.'

'If you do, make sure you use the credit card to pay for accommodation.'

'I can manage,' Kelly said with a smile.

'I'm sure you can but since you are going over for supplies and building materials I think that classes as a work-related trip.'

Kelly shrugged and seemed content to let it go.

'I have put some individual meals in the freezer so you should be all right for dinner if I'm not back.'

'I'll be fine,' Olivia said with a smile of her own. 'I lived here for months before you and survived.'

Kelly raised an eyebrow. He didn't need to voice his thoughts that she might have survived but certainly hadn't been taking good care of herself. She had only been eating Kelly's home-cooked meals for a week but she could already feel herself filling out a bit, and not in a bad way.

She had lost a lot of weight and it had not been a good look. But she wasn't sure she was ready to acknowledge out loud that Kelly's presence had made such a difference to her life.

There was still a week to run on their trial period and she wanted to make sure she was certain before agreeing to him taking the permanent position. For his part, Kelly hadn't brought up the subject and Olivia was happy to wait for another week before having that conversation.

'It will be a day, and maybe a night. Mabel and I will do just fine,' she assured him.

'Great, well I'll let you know,' Kelly said before hauling a rucksack on to his shoulder and leaving the kitchen. Olivia watched him go and Mabel whined.

'He'll be back later,' she told the dog, although now that Kelly was actually leaving, Olivia wasn't so sure she liked the idea, either. Having someone to help out had worked out much better than she expected.

Kelly had kept to his word and left her to her painting, interrupting only if she had gone too many hours without eating. He was an excellent cook and was making great strides with fixing up the run-down house.

And she had to admit to herself, it was nice to have some company, company that was very much on her own terms.

Olivia found it harder to get lost in her painting. She had one ear out for the phone. The weather outside was a little stormy and so she spent much of her time staring outside and wondering if Kelly and Derek would be able to make the boat trip back.

Kelly hadn't rung, which was a good sign, but it was also past lunchtime and if he was coming back he would need to head over soon to avoid low tide. Mabel had been restless, too, and paced up and down.

'Why don't we take a stroll down to

the beach?' Olivia asked the dog who looked up and sniffed the air.

'We can take the phone with us so if Kelly does ring we won't miss him. It would be good to stretch our legs,' Olivia added as Mabel gave her knowing look as if she suspected her true motives.

Down on the beach they would be able to see if Derek's small boat was cutting through the waves and be there to meet Kelly.

'Perhaps we should take the trolley just in case? I suspect Kelly will be bringing over lots of things that will need carrying up to the house.'

Olivia grabbed the trolley handle. Mabel jumped in and sat upright, like royalty going for a ride. Olivia laughed and headed towards the beach tugging the trolley behind them.

They made their way along the path and Olivia could see that sea was choppy, the waves running high up the beach and then crashing back out to sea. Mabel's ears were flapping in the wind and she whined.

47

'I don't think he's going to make it, either,' Olivia said, looking down to the small jetty which was being battered by the high seas. She didn't think the boat would be able to tie up safely and even if it could, walking the jetty would be near impossible. As if Kelly could read her thoughts the phone rang in her pocket and Olivia pulled it out.

'Olivia?' His voice crackled as if he were much further away than the mile or so that separated the island from the mainland.

'Kelly? Sorry — hard to hear you.'

'The line's not good,' he replied. 'I'm really sorry but Derek says it's not safe to make it back today.'

'Not a problem. I figured as much,' Olivia said, forcing herself to sound cheerful. She didn't want to admit that her heart had sunk as soon as she had heard the phone ring. She needed some time to think about her reaction and she didn't want to make Kelly feel bad or that she was so needy that could no longer cope with a night alone.

'Derek is going to bring me across as soon as the tides are favourable tomorrow, so about eleven? The forecast says the weather should clear by the morning.'

'Have you sorted out somewhere to stay?' Olivia asked.

'Derek is going to put me up.'

Olivia rolled her eyes — anything, it seemed, to avoid spending her money which she supposed she should be grateful for.

'Well, make sure you take him out to dinner on me,' Olivia said.

'Actually, I was going to cook.'

Of course you were, Olivia thought.

'Well, at least buy him a bottle of whisky.'

'Will do,' Kelly said and Olivia was sure he was grinning from the tone of his voice.

'Great, have a good evening.'

'See you tomorrow and don't forget to eat this evening.'

'I won't,' Olivia said, rolling her eyes and hoping that the expression was somehow translated in her own tone of voice.

She hung up and pushed the phone back in to her pocket. The wind was starting to pick up and Mabel was now crouched low in the trolley.

'All right, back home for us and we'll batten down the hatches,' she told Mabel and set off briskly back to the house.

With lamb stew defrosting in a pan on the stove and the curtains closed, Olivia could almost forget that there was a storm raging outside.

It wasn't even the worst storm she had experienced on the island. Several before had brought down trees, not to mention tiles from the aged roof. She had survived those on her own with only Mabel for company but even Mabel seemed a little bit on edge. Had they both become soft after only a week, Olivia asked herself crossly.

She scooped Mabel up in her arms.

'We'll be fine. We've been through worse,' Olivia told Mabel, although she wasn't sure who she was trying to convince.

The words had barely left her mouth when there was the sound of smashing glass. Mabel barked and then tried to bury her head inside Olivia's jumper.

'You are going to have to stay in here,' Olivia said firmly. 'It sounds like there will be some broken glass and we don't want you cutting your paws. One emergency at a time.'

Olivia put Mabel in her basket and then closed the kitchen door behind her. She knew at least one window had been broken as she stepped into the hall. It was as if the storm had been invited into the house. Wind seemed to howl around every corner and the temperature had dropped from the cosiness of the kitchen with its wood stove.

The front door was closed and the glass intact and so Olivia moved across to her small office. There were no signs of disruption here and so she headed for the lounge. Again, everything seemed fine but Olivia's heart dropped. It could mean only one thing. The broken glass was in her studio.

Her mind raced as she tried to remember whether she had wrapped all the paintings for sending to Abby. She raced for the door and yanked it open. It wasn't easy as she was fighting against the wind. Stepping into the studio felt like it was right in the middle of the storm.

The wind swirled around, picking up everything and making it dance in mini tornadoes. Paper and brushes and sketches flew through the air. Her easels had been cast aside and the tubes of paint and brushes were scattered across the floor. As lightning flashed across the sky she could see the heavy branch that had been picked up and thrown through the wall of glass like a toddler having a tantrum.

For a heartbeat Olivia stood there not knowing what to do, what to try and rescue first. It was the worst kind of destruction and she had to deal with it alone. She felt paralysed and then a voice jolted through her head. No-one was coming to rescue her, not tonight and she needed to do something.

She took a step forward, glass breaking under her feet and grabbed the nearest painting. It had fallen from its easel but it looked as though it hadn't been harmed by the weather. She took it to the hall and placed it against the wall before returning to the wreck of her studio.

Half an hour later and Olivia had managed to rescue all that was worth saving. Several paintings were beyond salvaging but to her relief, the ones she had wrapped up were safe. She had managed to pull some paints, brushes and one easel from the mess. The rest looked ruined beyond repair in the half light.

Her hair was stuck to her scalp and she was soaked through and shivering. She could hear Mabel scrabbling at the kitchen door as she pulled the studio door to, and locked it. She had thought about trying to find a covering for the broken window but it didn't seem worth it. The weather had done its damage and she didn't think it could get any worse.

She opened the door to the kitchen and Mabel shot out and threw herself into Olivia's arms.

'It's OK, Mabel. The same can't be said for my studio but look, I managed to rescue a few paintings.'

Olivia buried her face in Mabel's fur and tried not to think about the state of her studio.

'There's nothing we can do about it now so I think a hot bath and some supper are in order before an early night.'

Just as Olivia uttered those words there was a fizz and a pop and all the lights went out. Olivia groaned and went in search of the emergency candles and matches.

★ ★ ★

Olivia was awake as the sun came up. She hadn't really been able to sleep. All she could think about was the work that she had lost and the damage to her studio.

Mabel was curled beside her fast asleep

54

which was not surprising since Olivia's tossing and turning had kept the little dog awake most of the night, too. Olivia tried to ease herself out of bed without disturbing Mabel but as her feet hit the ground her dog was by her side.

'I'm going to go and take a look,' Olivia said. 'Maybe it won't be as bad as I thought.'

She quickly pulled on some clothes and then headed downstairs, Mabel at her feet. Sun was shining through every window in the kitchen as if the storm of the night before were just a bad dream but the piles of slightly bedraggled paintings and tumble of art supplies told Olivia otherwise. She scooped Mabel up into her arms.

With a deep breath she unlocked the studio door and pushed it open.

The tree branch seemed smaller than it had last night but it was still where the wind had left it, half in and half out the glass wall, taking four panes with it.

There was broken glass everywhere, along with soggy sheets of paper, some blank and some with drawings on. The floor which was cream tiles was covered in streaks of oil paint. To Olivia it looked as if the storm itself had tried its hand at painting. It was a mess and it was going to take time and money to fix.

A Helping Hand

Olivia had made breakfast and drunk some coffee before taking Mabel out for a walk and then she knew she couldn't put it off any longer. The electricity was back on and she knew she probably ought to contact Abby to tell her what had happened and to work out what paintings could still be sold.

First she needed to survey the damage to her precious studio and attempt to clear up. A glance at her watch told her that she had a few hours before Kelly would be back and she didn't want to give the impression that she was completely helpless.

Olivia had swept the glass up into one pile of shards. Some of the panes had broken into large pieces and so would need carefully removed from the frames but she would do that later. First of she wanted to make the floor safe so that she could let Mabel roam about without risking cutting her paws. Mabel was whining outside the closed door and had been for the last hour and Olivia wasn't sure how much more of it she could take.

'Mabel!' she called through the closed door, 'I can hear you and as soon as I have swept up this mess, I promise I will let you back in!'

With the dustpan in one hand and the brush in the other, Olivia started to collected up the tiny pieces before emptying them into a sturdy cardboard box she had found. Mabel's barking made her jump just as she was about to pick up a much larger piece of glass.

Olivia sucked in some air as the edge of the glass went deep into her thumb. She dropped the piece of glass and watched in slow motion as is shattered into hundreds of small pieces.

'Olivia?' a voice called and it sounded concerned.

'Watch the glass!' Olivia shouted as the door opened but to her relief, Kelly had scooped Mabel up into his arms. Kelly's eyes swept the room and then settled on Olivia and the blood that was now dripping from her thumb.

'You're bleeding,' he said, stepping into the room.

Olivia looked back at her thumb and it seemed to register for the first time. The lack of sleep, the state of her beautiful studio, her lost work and the blood slowly dripping from her thumb all suddenly seemed too much and she could feel herself sway on her feet. Her mind barely registered Kelly's arms making a grab for her before lifting her up as if she weighed nothing.

The next thing she knew, she was on the sofa in the lounge and Kelly was wrapping a bandage around her thumb.

'You're lucky it's not too deep. I've pulled the edges together with steri-strips and as long as you keep it dry, it will be fine.'

Olivia nodded as she tried to make sense of what had just happened.

'I'm fine,' she said, forcing herself to sit up. 'I'm not normally squeamish,' she added, feeling the need to point that out to Kelly, who just smiled.

'Looks like you've had quite a night. I'm not surprised you had a little wobble.'

Olivia nodded, checking his face for any signs that he was being patronising — that, she didn't think she could bear. But his smile was open and warm and most of all genuine.

'I'm sorry I wasn't here to help out. I got back this morning as soon as possible.'

'We were fine,' Olivia said as Mabel jumped up and licked her nose. 'I just rescued what I could last night and locked the door. The power went off so I couldn't see to do anything more.'

'How are your paintings?' he asked as he used a piece of tape to hold the bandage in place.

'Thankfully I had some already wrapped to be shipped to Abby but I lost a few.'

'I'm sorry to hear that. I should have taken some branches off those trees.'

Olivia laughed.

'The trees are so far away from the

60

house it never would have occurred to me that they could do damage to the studio. And it certainly isn't your fault,' she added as she recognised the look on Kelly's face. It seemed he was the sort of person who took the blame for anything that went wrong, as if somehow he could be blamed for an act of nature.

'Well I'll get a tarp up so if it does rain again the place won't flood. I can start measuring for panes of glass. I should be able to get it fixed up.'

'Good. I need to sort through and work out what I can save and what will need to go to the tip.' She frowned at the thought. Getting rid of rubbish was not easy on the island, as it all had to go by boat to the mainland.

'I think you are going to need to be site supervisor and direct me.'

Olivia raised an eyebrow. Was he suggesting she wasn't capable? Just because she had gone a bit light-headed didn't mean she couldn't look after herself.

'Relax, Olivia. I don't mean you can't do it. I just think you need to be careful of that thumb. If it opens up again you may need stitches.'

Olivia felt some of the tension leave her.

'Fine. I will be careful and you can move any of the big stuff.'

'Deal. But first you need to eat and drink something. I left most of the building stuff back with Derek. He's going to bring it over later. I brought some Cornish pasties with me for lunch.'

Olivia knew that Kelly was right. The fact that she had skipped breakfast probably hadn't helped her wobble. Mabel started to do her little dance which meant she was hungry, too. It looked like Olivia was outnumbered and so she nodded before slowly getting to her feet.

'Sounds like a plan,' she said.

They worked through the afternoon and by the time the light was starting to fade, they had cleared all of the rubbish and salvaged what they could. Kelly had measured up for the wood and glass he would need to complete the repairs and Olivia had scrubbed the tiled floor with her good hand to little effect.

'I kind of like it,' Kelly said, taking in the splattered flooring. 'It seems very arty to me.' He grinned at Olivia.

Olivia frowned. Since she had owned the house and the studio she had tried to change as little as possible. There were things that had needed fixing but she wanted to keep the essence of the house the same. She wasn't sure if it was that she wanted to honour the artist's memory or if she was superstitious that if she changed too much she would lose the ability to paint anything that anyone would want to buy.

'But if you don't like it I can see if I can get something that will take up the paint?'

Olivia started as she realised that Kelly was talking to her.

'I don't know,' Olivia said, staring at the floor. 'Maybe it's part of the studio's journey.' She felt her cheeks burn when she realised she had said it out loud. Talking about the studio as if it were a live entity was a sure way to convince

Kelly that she was a mad artist.

But Kelly chuckled and Olivia got the impression that he knew what she meant.

'Old houses have a soul, if you ask me. I rented a new build flat in London and it was like an empty box with no history. This place,' he said gesturing around the room, 'it's like you can feel all the people that have lived here before, almost like the house itself is alive and has a story to tell.'

Olivia looked at Kelly. If anyone else had said that she would have assumed that they were taking the mickey.

She knew that some of her ideas and thoughts were a bit 'out there' for most people. But she was also sure that was what made her a painter — the ability to see beyond what most people could see and capture something more on canvas.

'Now you sound like an artist,' she said with a smile and she knew in that moment that the painted floor was staying.

'I think I get it from my mum,' Kelly said and then turned away and busied himself measuring a window that Olivia was sure he had measured before.

'Was she an artist?' Olivia asked gently. Kelly had brought up the subject but she knew from her own experience that it didn't always mean that you wanted to talk about it.

'I don't really know,' Kelly replied, staring at the notebook that he had used to make a record of all the supplies he would need to repair the broken windows.

'My dad never really wanted to talk about her. I think it was just too painful for him and it felt wrong to ask him too many questions.'

Olivia nodded as Kelly looked up at her. He shrugged.

'But in so many ways I'm different from my dad so I always kind of figured it must be what I inherited from her.'

'Your dad doesn't cook, then?' Olivia asked with a smile. Kelly laughed.

'He's officially banned from the kitchen after letting a pan boil dry to the point it started to melt.' Kelly shook his head at the memory and Olivia laughed.

'Cooking is creative, just like painting. You have to have a kind of vision that other people can't see,' Olivia offered.

'I never really thought about it like that but you're right,' Kelly replied.

'So what's your dream? Open a restaurant? Earn some Michelin stars?' Olivia asked. If she were honest she wasn't any kind of expert when it came to food, other than knowing what she liked to eat.

'Yeah, but not in London; more like somewhere I could grow all my own food to cook. I want to make good food accessible and lose some of the pretension that comes with big city restaurants.'

Olivia nodded. Somehow she couldn't really see Kelly working at one of the posh restaurants she had been to. They weren't places she would have chosen. They were too formal and the food often too strange, not to mention the prices. That and the fact that she often came away feeling hungry. They just weren't her thing.

'You know, John who left this place to me left me a whole collection of photographs over the years. There was a thriving vegetable garden in the Twenties. We could reinstate it, if you like,' Olivia said, adding a shrug to show that she wasn't worried one way or the other.

Kelly looked at her.

'Does that mean that my two-week probation is over?' he asked and his face was unreadable. Olivia felt uncertain. She had been so focused on it being her decision whether he stayed or not, she hadn't even given a thought as to whether he would want to stay. Maybe he didn't.

'I mean, yes. If you want to stay? Don't feel any under pressure. I know that I wasn't sure when you first arrived.

'It was just a bit of a shock when I saw you and to be honest I wasn't certain if I could share this place. I thought you might stop me from painting and . . .' Olivia knew that she was gabbling but didn't seem to be able to stop herself.

Kelly was smiling broadly and Olivia had to look away, feeling both embarrassed at her reaction and relieved that it seemed highly likely Kelly was about to tell her that he was going to stay.

'I was hoping I might pass muster.'

'Well, you're a great cook and you leave me to it,' Olivia said, picking up the broom and giving the floor an unnecessary brush. 'So I think it is working, assuming you are happy here.'

'It's an amazing place, Olivia, and if you are happy for me to try out some new recipes on you then I think we have a deal. I need to create a portfolio of them before I can go to the bank and see about finance.'

Olivia didn't know why but the idea of Kelly leaving was suddenly causing an awful heaviness in her chest.

Just a matter of a week before she had insisted on a two-week trial period after which she knew she would feel less guilty telling Kelly that it hadn't worked out. But now Kelly was talking about leaving at some point and somehow she couldn't imagine the place without him.

'Great,' she managed to say, forcing a smile. Something she had a lot of practice in was not letting the pain show on her face.

Change of Scene

When the phone rang an hour after they had finished eating, Olivia knew who it was, despite the fact that it wasn't the regular call time and she also knew she was in trouble.

'Hi, Abby, how are you?' Olivia hoped that her light-hearted tone might convey that she was fine, despite the disasters that had befallen her.

'Me? What about you? Why am I just hearing about this now? I knew you shouldn't be left on that island alone!'

'Kelly told you, then?'

'He just sent me a text. I can't believe it. Why didn't you call me?'

'Well, firstly the phones were down and secondly I'm fine. Kelly is going to repair the window and I managed to salvage most of my paintings.'

Abby tutted down the phone and Olivia could imagine her waving the sentence away with a hand.

'I'm not worried about the paintings,'

she said, sounding exasperated. 'I'm worried about you.'

'Well, you don't need to be. I'm fine,' Olivia said firmly.

Olivia felt the pang in her chest return.

'Tell me you have decided that he should stay? After everything that's happened, Liv.'

'Of course. He's agreed to stay.' She wanted to add the 'for now' but she didn't think she could bear to speak about the possibility of Kelly leaving. She wasn't ready to say it out loud.

'Good,' Abby said, sounding a little surprised. 'Now do you need to send me any paintings? If there is water damage I might be able to get our restorer to have a look at them.'

Olivia gave an internal sigh of relief. At least now they could move on to safer ground.

* * *

The end of the two-week trial period passed in a bit of a blur. Olivia had sent

71

her salvaged paintings to Abby, who had been really pleased with them and told her to get painting more. Kelly had fixed up the studio in a matter of days and was now dividing his time between fixing up the rest of the house and cooking delicious food.

Olivia had pushed the idea that Kelly would one day leave to the back of her mind. She told herself firmly that she was being foolish and besides, she had no idea what her own life would look like in six months' time. She might be ready for a change by then herself.

The smell of freshly baked pastries was wafting through the house and since Olivia had taken to wedging open the door to her studio, she was not immune.

Mabel liked to divide her time between Olivia and Kelly and Olivia had tired of having to step away from her work to open the door to let her in and out. Kelly was still leaving her to it, unless it was very late and she had completely forgotten to eat.

With her stomach rumbling and a

strong desire for a cup of tea, she stepped away from her latest painting. Some wildflowers had sprung up in what used to be the back garden of the house and Olivia had spent some time sketching them in the sunshine before coming back indoors to paint but now she was ready for tea and, from the smell of it, something delicious to eat.

Mabel was curled up in her basket snoring as Kelly pulled a tray of cinnamon rolls from the oven.

'Perfect timing,' he said, placing them on the table to cool. 'I've just made tea and these are best fresh from the oven.'

Olivia took a seat at the table and looked out of the kitchen window which was open to the breeze. Outside she could see that Kelly had marked out a piece of land and started to dig.

'You've been busy,' she said, accepting a mug of tea.

Kelly glanced over his shoulder.

'I thought I'd get started on reclaiming the vegetable garden. I checked out the photos and so I think I'm in the right spot for the kitchen garden.'

'Looks like it. I'm happy to help with planting,' she added, taking a sip of tea.

'Only if you have your painting done.'

'You sound like Abby,' Olivia said, smiling, 'and as I keep telling her, artists need to find inspiration away from the canvas as much as they need to spend time actually drawing and painting.'

'Noted.' Kelly smiled back before taking a couple of buns from the hot pan and putting them on a plate. 'Careful — they're still pretty hot.'

Kelly and Olivia dug into the buns.

'These are amazing,' she said with a full mouth. Kelly smiled and handed her a napkin.

'You have cinnamon on your chin.'

'You could definitely sell these,' she said before wiping at her chin and taking another bite.

'Funny you should say that. I've been working on a picnic package. You know, one that people could come in and buy on the day they want to go out.'

'If these are part of it, you are on to a

winner.'

'They are, but so are pork pies, freshly baked rolls and other nibbles.'

'Sounds delicious and a great idea.'

'In that case, can I interest you in a test run?'

'You never have to ask me to try your food, Kelly,' Olivia said, laughing.

'No, but a true test run would involve an actual picnic, and it is Sunday tomorrow. I was wondering if you would like to come out to the point with me?'

Olivia looked up and he looked her straight in the eye. She blinked and nodded, feeling more than a little dazzled.

'Maybe you will find some inspiration out there for a new painting,' he added.

'Maybe,' she said before taking another bite of the bun to keep herself from having to say anything more.

Her mind was racing with possibilities that went beyond simple food tasting. Maybe Kelly wanted them to spend some more time together? She knew she had moved from not wanting him around to kind of craving his company.

The problem was she wasn't sure if it was just because he was the only other person on the island or if it was because it was him.

He was warm and friendly, not to mention kind and handsome, but he also had plans. Plans which involved leaving the island and her behind.

No, her heart had been broken before and she wasn't about to risk it again on someone who had made it clear that he would be leaving at some point. He was just being friendly and there was nothing wrong with that, she told herself firmly.

★   ★   ★

Olivia woke from her weekly lie-in to find she was alone in bed. Judging from the sounds in the kitchen, Kelly was hard at work which meant that was where Olivia would find Mabel.

Olivia took her time getting up. Once out of the shower she needed to decide what she was going to wear. The problem was she couldn't remember the last time she had worn anything other than her range of cargo trousers, at various stages of becoming completely covered in paint and the T-shirts that went with them, in an equally splattered state.

It wasn't that she didn't have clothes — her wardrobe was full of them — it was just that it felt like choosing the wrong clothes might give the wrong impression.

She wanted to look nice, it was a day off and they were going for a picnic but she didn't want to look as though she was trying too hard. It was ridiculous how much she was over-thinking this.

Less than two weeks ago she had been locked into her new life, one of solitude and she realised now, wallowing in grief. The idea of meeting someone new was so outrageous she would have laughed out loud, not a happy laugh but a dry, broken one.

But now it seemed, the first man to appear in her life was turning her head. She stared at herself in the mirror. She still wore the necklace and the ring that hung from it.

Perhaps it was because she knew Kelly was leaving so it was almost safe to dally with the idea of meeting someone new, knowing that it had no future and so could remain a dream, an idea in her head.

Perhaps that's how healing worked? You needed to start somewhere so an imaginary relationship meant you could get used to the idea without actually risking your heart?

Olivia shook her head at her reflection. She was being ridiculous. Kelly was a friend and she was helping him out tasting his new picnic food. That was all there was to it and taking hours to choose her outfit meant she was behaving like a teenager.

She grabbed a pair of trousers and a black top. She would look casual and relaxed but not as though she had made a great effort. A perfect choice. There was a soft scrabbling at the door and Mabel bounced in. She was hopping from foot to foot and looking from Olivia to the door.

'OK, I get the message. You are both ready and I am holding things up.' Olivia couldn't help but smile. She walked towards the door and watched Mabel fly down the stairs as fast as her short legs could carry her.

Kelly stepped out from the kitchen with a regulation army backpack over one shoulder.

'Morning,' Kelly said with a smile. 'I hope Mabel didn't wake you?'

'I was up and besides I'm not sure you should feel the need to apologise for my dog,' Olivia added with a smile.

'I scouted the best place on the island, unless you have somewhere in mind?'

Olivia shook her head.

'The island is only a kilometre long and less than that wide so there aren't that many places to choose from.'

Kelly opened the door and let Olivia and Mabel out before him.

Outside the sun was working its way up to its peak and it felt warm on Olivia's skin. There was a breeze coming off the sea which meant even if it was going to be hot they would still be comfortable. Kelly pulled the door closed behind him. Olivia rarely bothered to lock it since they were the only people on the island.

She followed Kelly along the narrow path with Mabel running circles around them. She didn't go to the south side of the island all that much as it was more prone to high winds and poor weather, without the nearby shelter of the mainland.

The path in the grass looked as if it had been there for hundreds of years and as they neared the sea, it widened out and Olivia and Kelly were able to walk side by side.

'I found this spot last week and it's a great place to watch ships out at sea,' he said, turning to her, and she could see her own love of the island reflected in his eyes. It was like sharing a secret place with someone and she felt more drawn to him than ever.

'It's a bit rocky getting down there but there's a great flat stone that we can sit on.'

The climb down was a bit of a scramble but Olivia took it slowly and made it safely to the bottom.

Kelly's spot was a small cove that was perhaps only 40 feet wide and, by the looks of it, would be swallowed by the sea at high tide. There was a low flat rock above the waterline and the sea had receded to reveal some rock pools which Mabel was now busily exploring.

Kelly put down his rucksack and pulled out a picnic blanket that he spread over the rock before reaching out a hand to help Olivia up on to the rock.

'I had no idea this was here,' Olivia said, looking out to sea.

'I think I was just lucky that I was passing when the tide was at its lowest. We need to keep a close eye on the sea. We have a few hours but when it turns it happens quickly.'

He started to pull plastic boxes from his rucksack and handed Olivia a flask.

'Fresh coffee, if you wouldn't mind doing the honours?'

Olivia poured the coffee into two plastic mugs.

'I hope you're hungry?' Kelly asked and Olivia nodded enthusiastically.

'No breakfast.'

Kelly laid out a veritable feast of homemade goodies and they tucked in.

'Well?' he asked after they had eaten in silence for some time. 'You can be honest,' he added and Olivia could see genuine anxiety on his face.

'Delicious,' Olivia said, licking her fingers after sampling a sweet pastry filled with cherries.

Kelly beamed.

'Anything that you think needs improving?'

'I already told you everything was delicious,' Olivia said with a smile.

'I know but I need constructive criticism if I'm going to develop this into a product.'

Olivia nodded and tried to think of something to say. She had been so lost in the beautiful scenario, the company and the food that she hadn't really taken each dish in turn and analysed it.

'The pickle in the sandwiches was a little sharp,' she said, looking carefully at Kelly's face. There was a flash of something but then he smiled.

'I mean, I like it like that but some people might expect something sweeter,' Olivia added hurriedly. The last thing she wanted to do was upset Kelly.

'It's fine, Olivia. This is good,' he said, pulling a small notebook from his rucksack and scribbling in it. 'What about the salmon puffs?'

They took each dish in turn and discussed it. Olivia found herself enjoying the conversation. These days she didn't have much opportunity to talk to people.

She had thought she was comfortable with that but actually it was nice, as was taking some time out. Her eyes were drawn to the view of the sea and the pattern of the jagged rocks. Without saying a word, Kelly pulled a small sketch book from his bag and handed it over with a small tin of charcoal that Olivia kept for outings.

'I'll go and play with Mabel,' he said with a grin before standing up and whistling for the dog.

Olivia watched them play and made a few quick sketches. She didn't normally paint things other than landscape or still life but there was something so joyous about the pair racing each other up and down that Olivia knew she would want to commit it to canvas at some point.

Once she had her sketches she turned to the view and got lost in it. The next thing that Olivia was aware of was the crash of a huge wave over her head.

No More Heartbreak

For a split second she thought she was drowning but as suddenly as it had arrived, it was gone. She had managed to keep hold of her sketch book but the stick of charcoal she had in her hand was nowhere to be seen.

Kelly's rucksack, which he had repacked, had slid to the very edge of the flat rock and was in danger of being washed away. Olivia climbed to her feet and made a grab for it.

'Olivia!' She heard the shout. 'Olivia, are you OK?'

Olivia nodded but couldn't find the breath to make words. The day might be warm but the sea was icy cold. Slipping and sliding she made her way to the edge of the flat rock and stepped down on to the beach, where a hand was waiting for her.

'I'm so sorry. Mabel ran off and I went after her. I should have paid more attention to the tide.'

'So should I,' Olivia said with a grin, through the chattering of her teeth. 'Where's Mabel?' she asked, scanning around and feeling panic. The little dog could swim but she would be no match for the strong current on this side of the island.

'I made her stay at the top before I came down for you,' Kelly said, taking the soggy rucksack from her hand and pulling it over his shoulder. 'Are your sketches ruined?' he added and there was a weight of guilt in his voice.

Olivia looked down at them.

'I think I can rescue them if I dry them out. And really they are just there to prompt my memory. I'll draw them again once we get back.'

Kelly held out a hand and Olivia took it and he helped her back up the slope, not easy since her shoes were soaked through and not giving the best grip.

At the top of the hill, Olivia expected him to draw his hand away but he didn't — he just kept walking. Olivia tried not to smile. She had to admit it

86

was nice to be close to someone after all her time alone and somehow it felt natural with Kelly.

Then Olivia remembered . . . Kelly was going to leave. Maybe not in the next few months but at some point he would be gone and she wasn't sure she could take more heartbreak.

Gently she pulled her hand free and disguised the action by reaching down to fuss Mabel's ears. Kelly looked at the place where her hand had been but said nothing.

Olivia didn't want to ruin what had been a perfect day, even with her shock soaking but at the same time she knew what she was doing was right. Ultimately she was protecting them both.

They walked back in silence. Olivia tried to think of something to say but couldn't think of anything and Kelly, usually the easy conversationalist, said nothing. It wasn't the comfortable silence that they had shared before and Olivia felt sad that it had to be that way but better to feel some pain now than complete heartbreak later.

'I can put your sketch book on the stove to dry,' Kelly offered, pushing open the front door.

There was a small smile on his face and Olivia felt herself relax a little. Perhaps they could go back to how they had been before? Relaxed friends, with nothing else on the table.

Olivia hurried upstairs and stripped off her soaked clothes before jumping in the shower. She pulled on a pair of comfortable painting trousers and a T-shirt before bundling her clothes in to a pile and carrying them back downstairs.

The previous owner of the house had converted the scullery into a sort of utility room and Olivia pushed her pile of wet clothes into the washing machine and set it to wash. She padded back into the kitchen. There was no sign of Kelly but a note left on the kitchen table.

'I'll be working in the vegetable garden if you need me. Sketch book should be dry. Supper at eight, if that suits?'

Olivia picked up the note and stared

at it, trying to work out if things had returned to normal or if Kelly was put out that she had pulled away. But the longer she stared at the note the more her mind came up with scenarios that involved Kelly abruptly packing his rucksack and leaving.

She moved over to the small kitchen window and could see Kelly digging over the earth and pulling up great handfuls of weeds, with Mabel by his side.

The best thing she could do now was see what sketches she could salvage.

* * *

There was a soft knock at the door and Olivia realised that the light in the studio was almost gone. She rubbed her eyes and turned to the door.

'Come in,' she called.

'Sorry to disturb you but it's almost eight. Is it all right if I start cooking?'

'I lost track of the time. I was sure I would be done way before now.'

'Can I have a look?' Kelly asked. He

walked over and looked at the array of sketches that she had completed, which covered the floor of the studio at her feet.

'May I?' he asked as he gestured at one. Olivia nodded. She was always nervous when people wanted to look at her work, afraid that they wouldn't like it.

'This is Mabel and me today?' he asked.

'I don't normally paint figures but you both seemed such a part of the landscape that I couldn't resist.'

'You're going to turn them into paintings?'

Olivia nodded and smiled as Kelly studied the sketch he held in his hand.

'You can have that one if you like,' she said, holding her breath and bracing herself for him to reject her offer. She wasn't sure why but she really wanted him to have it.

'I can't take this, but perhaps I can give you some money for it?'

'Don't be silly, I want you to have it.'

'But this is how you make your money, which would be like me making food and giving it away for free.'

'And I suppose you never do that for friends?' Olivia said, the word 'friends' feeling a little alien.

Kelly looked up from his close study of the sketch and she could feel his assessing gaze. She kept her expression light and hoped that she wasn't giving away her own, secret feelings.

She wanted him to take it. It felt like he would be taking a piece of her so that when he left, which she knew he was going to, he would have something to remind himself of the island and of her. And that was a comfort, somehow.

'I suppose I have, and there were a couple of people who were homeless near the restaurant and I used to open late so they could have at least one hot meal a day.'

That didn't surprise Olivia. She knew first-hand how generous he could be and he wasn't one of those people that talked about their kindness to get applause. It was just a comment in response to what she had said.

It made her heart yearn for him to stay even more. She wanted to get to know him better, to discover if there could be more between them but she pushed the thought down. Kelly needed to follow his dream as she had followed hers.

'If you are certain you can part with it, I would love to have it,' Kelly said, his expression soft, and Olivia knew that she was at risk of losing her heart once more.

'I'm certain,' she said, forcing her voice to stay steady. Kelly's eyes lit up.

'Then thank you.' Then he seemed to remember something and a change came over him. 'I'm cooking salmon and fresh veg for supper. Will you be ready in twenty minutes?'

'I'll just go wash up and I'll come and give you a hand.'

When Olivia walked into the kitchen, the table was laid and there was little for her to do. She wondered if she would be able to cope going back to ready meals when Kelly went off on his next adventure.

Kelly swiftly dished up baked salmon,

new potatoes, asparagus and carrots, before placing a small jug on the table, which from the smell of it was some kind of lemon sauce.

'I wish I could cook like this,' Olivia said before realising that she had said it out loud.

'I can teach you, if you like,' Kelly said, taking the seat opposite Olivia.

'You might want to rethink that — both my grandma and my dad have tried. I just get so flustered and can't remember what I am supposed to do next, even with a recipe.'

'I can diagnose your problem,' Kelly said with a smile.

'Really?' Olivia asked, smiling back.

'Cooking is an art, not a science. Sure, there are some elements of science in it but you need to see it more like a painting.'

'I hadn't thought of it like that.'

'It's as much about gut feelings as it is about following a recipe. Food talks to you if you listen.'

Olivia had been with him up to that

point but his last comment made a child-like giggle rise up inside her but Kelly didn't seem offended.

'You're not the first to tell me that I am a little obsessed with cooking.'

'Yeah, I was with you but listening to food talk was just a step too far.' She grinned at him and he grinned back.

'That's not exactly what I meant. More that you can, for example, tell if a cake is cooked by listening for bubbling. If it bubbles it's not done.'

'That makes sense, I suppose,' Olivia said, picking up her fork.

'Well, like I said the offer is there if you want to learn.'

Olivia looked up as Kelly focused on eating his supper. What harm could it do? It would be nice to spend some time together before he left and if he really could teach her the basics of cooking then that couldn't be a bad thing.

A First Time
for Everything

'Right, so yesterday we cooked a basic stew and I think we can both agree that it was delicious.'

Olivia nodded and could feel a glow of pride. Her first meal and she had aced it, not to mention the fact that she and Kelly had hung out for a couple of hours and she had really enjoyed his company.

'So tonight we are going to try something sweet.'

Olivia gulped and had a flashback to a particularly disastrous Home Economics lesson at school in which she had set fire to a tea-towel and burnt her chocolate brownies.

'A Victoria sandwich cake. It uses a basic cake recipe that you can use for all sorts of other cakes and once you can master this there will be a whole world of other bakes waiting for you.'

Kelly must have seen Olivia's unconvinced expression because he nudged her.

'Confidence, remember?' he said and all Olivia could do was hope that she wouldn't make a fool of herself.

Kelly had laid out all the ingredients on the kitchen table and set up a bowl, weighing scales and an electric hand mixer.

'Right first, I tend to weigh by eye but I think we should start with the scales, so weigh out the butter and sugar.'

Olivia did as she was instructed and dumped both into the bowl.

'Right, now we are going to cream them together using the mixer.'

Olivia nodded, picked up the mixer and pushed the on button. The lump of butter flew out of the bowl and hit the wall opposite. Neither she nor Kelly said anything as they watched it slide down the wall, before hitting the floor.

As soon as it was at ground level, Mabel was on it, licking it for all she was worth. Olivia grabbed Mabel and Kelly scooped up the lump of butter before wiping off the wall with a cloth.

'Sorry . . .' Olivia said, feeling redness rise up her chest and burn her cheeks.

'My fault, I should have said to make sure the mixer was on the lowest setting or . . .'

'Or the butter will launch itself into the air like a missile?'

'Something like that,' Kelly said with a grin. 'Maybe we should go old school and do it by hand?'

Olivia put Mabel back on her bed and washed her hands, wondering whether she would be able to mess up hand whisking.

Kelly measured out more butter and sugar and then handed Olivia a wooden spoon.

'First try a sort of mashing motion to soften up the butter and then work at getting the sugar all mixed in.'

Olivia poked at the lump of butter with the spoon. It seemed fairly solid so she tried to mash it flat in the bowl.

'Give it some welly,' Kelly said, pulling out a chair and sitting down.

Five minutes later and Olivia was red

faced again but this time with the effort. She had no idea how her granny had managed to continue baking well into her nineties. This was hard work! Worse than a session at the gym.

Her arms ached but at least the butter was no longer a solid lump. She showed the bowl to Kelly who was finding the whole thing far too amusing for Olivia's liking.

'That should about do it. Now we are going to slowly beat in the eggs.'

Kelly handed Olivia an egg and she stared at it. She had never been good at cracking open eggs and now didn't seem a very good time to practise. With a sigh she gently tapped the egg of the side of the bowl.

'Might need to try a bit harder if we want to bake this cake tonight,' Kelly said but his smile was gentle this time. Olivia took a deep breath and bashed the egg on the side of the bowl. It promptly collapsed into a mess of shell, yoke and white.

'No problem, we can fish those bits

out,' Kelly said, using a teaspoon to scoop out bits of shell.

'I told you I was hopeless,' Olivia said, wishing she had never started this whole thing. It was mortifying and Kelly must think she was an idiot.

'Nonsense. Nobody is any good at anything unless they practise. Try again,' he said, holding out the second egg. Olivia tried again and this time managed to get the egg in the bowl without the shell.

'See, I told you. Just practice.' Kelly handed Olivia the wooden spoon. 'Gently now.' Olivia did as she was told.

'Where did you learn to cook?' Olivia said, realising that she had never asked.

'I was pretty much left to my own devices in the evenings and got fed up with living on ready meals.'

Olivia looked up at him expecting sadness in his eyes but instead she saw something else. Kelly shrugged.

'I didn't have an easy time of it. My dad was pretty lost in his grief but it allowed me to discover baking and cooking. I used to watch all the programmes on TV and get recipe books out of the library.'

'My Home Economics teacher kept suggesting the same to me,' Olivia said as Kelly handed her the bowl of flour and a sieve.

'I didn't do Home Ec when I was at school and I didn't even tell anyone what I loved to do.'

They poured the cake mixture into the tin and Kelly open the oven door so that Olivia could put the tin in to bake.

'How about a cuppa?' Olivia said and hurried to do it before Kelly could step in. 'So why did you join the army, if cooking was your thing?'

'It seemed like a good place to learn the skills and to see a bit of the world.'

'And did you? See the world, I mean?'

'I saw more of it than I could have ever imagined,' Kelly said with a faraway look in his eyes.

'Not all of it good?' Olivia asked gently as she placed a steaming mug of tea in front of him.

'We did a lot of good,' he said in a tone

that suggested he was trying to remind himself of that, 'but there were many we couldn't help.'

Olivia didn't know what to say. Her life had been remarkably sheltered in comparison. Kelly looked up at her and smiled.

'Life is tough, that's one thing you learn and you have to grab happiness when you find it.'

Olivia felt a sudden lump appear in her throat. Without her realising it, happiness had crept up on her. It was something she hadn't thought possible and she wasn't sure she even wanted to be happy again but here she was.

Kelly had come into her life and his presence had made it better. She didn't spend every waking moment lost in the past any more — not to say she didn't still think about it but she had started to accept that life must go on.

'Hey, I'm sorry,' Kelly said and this time he was reaching for her. He cradled her hand in his and rubbed his thumb along the back of her hand.

'Don't be sorry.' She managed to say the words before she lost control of her emotions and found herself sobbing. Kelly moved to her side of the kitchen table and pulled her into his arms.

Olivia was used to crying but being held by someone she cared about was something she hadn't felt for what seemed like a lifetime. Kelly said nothing, just held her tightly. A buzzer sounded from the top of the stove.

'I think your cake is ready,' Kelly whispered and Olivia sat up, trying to remember how long it was supposed to take to cook. Had she really let herself be held for that long? What must Kelly think? She eased herself out of his embrace.

'Sorry,' she mumbled and moved towards the stove.

'No need to be,' he said, moving to stand beside her before handing her the oven gloves. 'Just open the door a peek and we'll see what it looks like.'

Olivia did as she was told, glad for the distraction. The cake had risen and was a soft golden brown.

'Looks perfect. Now take it out and place it on the top and we will do the skewer test.'

Olivia did as she was told and pushed the skewer into the centre of the cake, which came away clean.

'Congratulations, you have baked your first Victoria sponge.'

For a moment Olivia forgot what had just happened and felt herself beam with pride. She had to admit it looked good.

'When it's cool we'll cut it in half. I have some homemade strawberry jam for the middle that will do the trick.'

'Thank you,' Olivia said and she wasn't sure if she meant for the hug or the cake.

'I told you, everyone can bake with a bit of practice.' He smiled gently at her.

'And for the . . .' Olivia wasn't sure how to put into words what had happened. It was more than a hug, so much more.

It felt like the first real comfort she had had in a long time but there was no reason to think that Kelly thought of it as anything other than hugging a friend who was upset.

'Any time,' Kelly said. Mabel barked and it distracted Olivia long enough so that she couldn't dwell on his words or the expression on his face.

Mabel was scrabbling at the back door and was obviously in need of a leg stretch. It was the perfect excuse so she gave Kelly a small smile and opened the door.

'I'll just take Mabel out for a bit,' she said, stepping out without waiting for his reply and closing the door behind her.

Search in the Darkness

Olivia's mind was whirling around like autumn leaves caught in the wind. The sensation of being held would not go away nor would the idea that somehow she had stumbled upon happiness again without realising it had happened.

But these weren't her only thoughts. Kelly was going to leave at some point. He had said as much and she wasn't about stand in the way of his dreams. He had done so much for her and she didn't want to make him feel like she needed him so much he couldn't leave.

Olivia shook her head. No, that wasn't fair and she suspected he was exactly that kind of man. But if he stayed and those were his only reasons then one day he would resent her for it and she didn't think she could bear the thought of that.

Perhaps this was just the universe giving her a chance to move on, let go of the past and find her own happiness. Maybe Kelly had reminded her it was possible and she could now take steps by herself?

Mabel dashed off out of sight, barking. The sun had nearly set and it was difficult to make out the tiny shape in the half light.

'Mabel, stop chasing seagulls,' she called, laughing. Mabel tried but never succeeded but that never seem to put her off. Olivia continued walking.

'Mabel?' There was no answering bark or skitter of paws. 'Mabel!'

Olivia tried to take a calming breath. It wasn't like Mabel could get lost on the small island but that didn't explain why she had gone silent and disappeared.

Olivia was getting further and further from the house and more and more worried. It wasn't like Mabel to just run off and not come back when she was called.

Thoughts of anything else disappeared from her mind and all she could think of was Mabel, lost or maybe hurt and it made tears run down her cheeks. She didn't know what to do.

It was so much darker now that it was hard to make out anything. So she did the only thing she could. She ran back to the house. She would get a torch and some dog treats and come back out and search. Kelly would help her. Kelly would know what to do.

Olivia yanked open the back door to the kitchen but there was no sign of Kelly.

'Kelly? Kelly! I've lost Mabel!'

There was the noise of feet clattering down the stairs and Kelly appeared.

'Is she here?' Olivia asked, hoping that might be the answer.

'I haven't seen her and she wouldn't have been able to get in as the door was closed.'

Kelly moved to the pantry and found two torches before pushing his feet into the shoes he used for gardening.

'Don't worry, we'll find her.'

Olivia made to dash into the dark but a hand held her back.

'Slow down. We need to retrace your steps and listen out for her. If she is stuck somewhere we need to be able to call out and listen.'

Olivia nodded but it was dark and she doubted Kelly could see her but she felt him reach for her hand and she held on to it as if it were her lifeline.

'Let's take ten steps and then stop.'

Olivia did as she was told. It seemed a painfully slow way to find Mabel but she knew she wasn't thinking clearly in that moment. So they walked, stopped and called but there was no sign or sound. When they had retraced Olivia's steps she could feel her panic grow as if it were alive.

'Where is she?' Olivia shouted, her voice louder than she intended.

'We'll circle outwards from this point. It's the safest way to ensure we cover everywhere. She is here somewhere, there are only so many places to hide.'

'What if she's hurt?' Olivia asked as all sorts of images of Mabel in trouble crossed her mind.

'I'm sure she's fine but first we need to find her.'

Olivia allowed herself to be led in ever increasing circles, stopping every now and then to call Mabel's name but she was starting to lose hope. She knew that Mabel couldn't have got lost, and she also knew that Mabel would come when she was called, which only left dire scenarios.

'Maybe we should head back to the house? Perhaps she has found her way back there.'

'Shush,' Kelly said. Olivia went stock still and strained her ears but she could nothing but the wind blowing off the sea.

'This way,' Kelly said and headed off quickly in the direction of the sea. Olivia had to jog to keep up, one eye on the torch-lit uneven ground ahead of her and the other keeping track of Kelly's torchlight bouncing along as he started to run.

Kelly shouted something but it was lost in the wind. Olivia kept moving forward and felt the ground start to shift. She had hit the sand and could just make out the waves crashing in under the cloudy moon.

'Kelly?' she shouted, no longer able

to see his torch. She heard movement to her left and flashed her torch in that direction. A small body started to move towards her, barking and yelping. Olivia dropped her torch as Mabel launched herself into Olivia's arms.

'Where were you? Are you OK?' she asked the dog as if expecting her to answer. Olivia let the tears flow down her cheeks as she ran her hands over the little dog checking for injuries.

Other than the fact she was wet and smelled of rotting seaweed Olivia couldn't detect any injuries. She would take a closer look when they got Mabel back to the house and put her in a warm bath.

'I've got her, Kelly,' she called into the night. Mabel whined and Olivia felt the panic surge once more. Where was Kelly and why wasn't her answering her? Mabel wriggled in her arms, indicating she wanted to get down but Olivia wasn't quite ready to let her go just yet. She clipped Mabel's lead to her collar and gently put her down.

'Where's Kelly, Mabel? Do you know?'

As if she could understand every word, Mabel immediately started to pull Olivia in the direction that she had appeared from and Olivia hurried along behind her.

'Kelly?' Briefly Olivia wondered if Kelly was playing a joke on her. If he was, she was going to tell him exactly what she thought of him. After losing Mabel, this was not funny. But that thought was easier than the alternative. What had happened to Kelly? Was he hurt?

Mabel continued to tug on the lead and Olivia found herself leaving the sand and heading on to the uneven, slippery surface of the rock pools.

'Easy, Mabel. We won't be able to help him if we get hurt.'

Olivia slowed her pace, knowing what she had just said was true. If she sprained an ankle they would all be in serious trouble.

'Kelly?' she called but there was nothing but the sound of the wind. Mabel continued to tug and whine and Olivia struggled to keep her footing.

When Mabel suddenly stopped, Olivia could see nothing in the gloom until the wind suddenly blew the clouds away and revealed the moon.

There in the moonlight she could see a figure lying on the rocks . . . and it wasn't moving.

An Eventful Evening

In that moment Olivia felt frozen to the spot. She tried to call out Kelly's name but no words would come. Mabel barked and that seemed to be enough to shake Olivia from her shock. Carefully she crossed the distance between them. She looped Mabel's lead around her wrist, not wanting to risk her running off again and knelt down, ignoring the barnacles biting into her knees.

'Kelly?' she asked, reaching out a hand for his head. There was still no movement and Olivia felt the fear replaced by determination. She was going to help him, get him back to the house, call for help. Now was not the time to lose it, she needed to focus.

Beside Kelly's outstretched arm was the torch. It had gone out and Olivia reached for it, hoping that it wasn't broken. She pressed the button and the bulb lit up. She turned the torch on Kelly.

He was wet through and she could see

grazes along one leg where he had obviously taken a tumble but none of that would account for why he was lying so still.

She tried to remember what she had been taught at school about first aid and told herself firmly that as soon as she could she would go to a class and relearn anything she had forgotten.

She moved the torch to Kelly's face which was still as if he was asleep. She reached for his head and ran her hand around the back. She could feel a bump and knew that when he had taken a stumble he had obviously hit his head. She continued her inspection but apart from more scrapes she couldn't see any other injuries. His legs and arms seemed to be OK so she didn't think anything was broken.

'Right, Mabel, we need to figure out how to get Kelly off this beach,' Olivia said as the sea seemed to be creeping closer with every minute that passed. Mabel whined and leaned in to her. 'I know — but there must be a way.'

There was a moan and Olivia turned her attention back to Kelly.

'Kelly?'

Kelly groaned and moved.

'Take it easy. You slipped and bumped your head.'

Olivia watched as Kelly gingerly felt his head and moaned.

'There's no blood, just a bump, and I think you are going to have an almighty headache.'

'It's already started,' Kelly said, sounding groggy, but Olivia was just relieved that he was awake and talking.

'The tide is turning and we need to get you off the beach. Do you think you can stand if I help you?'

Kelly turned to look at her for the first time.

'Mabel?' he asked.

Olivia didn't need to answer as Mabel clambered over Kelly so that she could lick his face.

'Hey, girl. Glad you found your mum.'

'She's fine but right now we need to worry about you.'

'Ah, I've had worse,' Kelly said, trying to get to his feet. He staggered to the left so badly that Olivia was worried she wouldn't be able to keep him upright.

'I expect you have but now is not the time to play the hero,' she replied, slipping his arm around her shoulders. 'One step at a time.'

Olivia wasn't sure how they managed it. Kelly was leaning on her heavily and seemed to be struggling to keep on his feet. Mabel led the way, seeming to know that they needed to navigate the safest and shortest route off the rocks and on to solid ground.

'Do you need to rest?' Olivia asked, trying to catch her breath.

'I think if I stop I may not get up again,' Kelly said.

'Right, back to the house and then you can lie down.'

They took it slowly and Olivia kept glancing at Kelly nervously. He was pale and sweating and each step seemed a real effort.

When the lights of the house came into

116

view, Olivia felt like crying with relief but she knew it wasn't over yet. She needed to get Kelly some help and fast.

Olivia managed to manoeuvre Kelly on to the sofa. He lay full length with his eyes closed. Olivia went to the kitchen and pulled some ice from the freezer before wrapping it in a tea towel. She grabbed the phone and headed back to the lounge. Kelly opened his eyes as she walked in.

'Thanks,' he said as she took the home-made ice pack and pressed it gently against the side of his head.

'I should be the one thanking you. You found Mabel and got hurt in the process.'

'It's just a small bump. Is she OK?'

'She seems fine. I'm going to call the out-of-hours doctor and see if I can get someone to come and see you.'

'I doubt they'll to want to cross by boat and I don't think a bump to the head warrants a helicopter,' Kelly said, managing a smile.

'You knocked yourself out and I don't

know how long for.'

'Not long. I was just a bit stunned.'

Olivia raised an eyebrow and Kelly shrugged as if he realised that there was no way he was going to be able to stop her. Olivia moved out in the hall to make the call but stayed where she could keep an eye on Kelly. Mabel was curled up on his chest and Kelly was fussing her ears.

The doctor asked Olivia lots of questions and she had to act as an intermediary asking some of Kelly.

At the end of the conversation, the doctor advised Olivia to keep a close eye on Kelly and to call back if there was any change in his condition but he felt that a check-up could wait till morning. Olivia thanked the doctor and hung up. A small grin was playing across Kelly's face and Olivia glared at him.

'Told you. And as I said I've had worse.'

'Don't look so happy, the doctor has advised that I wake you up every hour just to check on you.'

'Ah, you don't need to do that. I have

a hard head.'

'I'm going to follow the instructions and in the morning, we are going to go over to the mainland and get the doctor to check you out.'

Kelly seemed to realise that there was, once again, no point in arguing and so he shrugged.

'Well, if it is going to be an all-nighter, why don't we have a coffee and some of your cake?'

Olivia felt some of the tension leave her. Kelly was looking better, there was more colour in his cheeks now he had been lying down for a while.

He was right, something to eat and drink would probably help both of them. It had been quite an evening and they were probably both in a bit of shock.

'Jam's in the fridge. Just put the sponge on its side and cut it in half. Spread the jam on the bottom half and then put the top half on.'

'Shout if you need anything,' Olivia said, feeling like she didn't want to leave him but knowing that they both could do with something to eat.

Olivia carried the cake and tray of coffee back into the lounge. She would never admit it to anyone but she was very pleased with her cake. It had risen beautifully and was a golden brown colour. With home-made strawberry jam inside, it looked delicious.

Mabel was snoozing on Kelly's chest in exactly the same position she had been in when Olivia left the room. Kelly had his eyes closed but something told her he wasn't asleep.

'Coffee?' she asked softly.

'Please — but I don't want to disturb her majesty,' Kelly said, opening his eyes.

Olivia laughed softly.

'She's going to have a rude awakening as she is going in the bath. I don't think either of us want to live with that smell any longer than we have to.'

Kelly made a show of sniffing Mabel's coat and then pulling a face.

'That is one smelly dog.'

'Where was she?' Olivia said, resting the tray on the low table and adding some sugar to Kelly's tea. She was sure that was what you were supposed to do for shock.

'She'd got herself tangled up in some fishing line. So much so that she couldn't move her back legs at all. She'd obviously panicked.'

Olivia nodded, taking this in and thinking that maybe she would walk the beach in daylight and make sure that there were no more fishermen's traps to catch her dog.

'And what happened to you?' she asked, looking curiously at Kelly. His face coloured a little and Olivia took a sip of hot coffee to disguise her smile.

'I freed Mabel and then she must have heard you because she dashed off. I made a grab for her but lost my balance.'

Olivia nodded, losing the battle with her smile.

'I know, I know,' Kelly said ruefully, 'I have trekked through some of the most dangerous parts of the world but I managed to slip in seaweed on this little slice of heaven and knock myself out.'

'I'm just glad you are OK,' Olivia said, looking more serious now. Joking aside, they had both been very lucky. Kelly could have done himself some serious injury.

'You scraped your knees, too,' Kelly said pointing at her knees which were streaked with thin grazes.

'Not as bad as yours. We probably should get those cleaned up,' Olivia said, leaning in to take a closer look.

'Cake first,' Kelly said, wriggling to sit up. Mabel grumbled but shifted with him so she was sitting on his lap.

'I think Mabel is feeling a little guilty,' Olivia said as she cut Kelly a large slice of cake.

'It wasn't the smartest thing you've ever done,' Kelly said, lifting the small dog up so that he could speak directly to her. Mabel licked his nose and Kelly smiled. 'I think maybe I should wash my hands before I eat.'

Gently he put Mabel to one side and eased himself to his feet. He wobbled a bit and Olivia made a grab for him.

'I'm fine,' he said but Olivia wasn't convinced and even if she were, she wasn't about to let him fall again.

'I'll come with you, no arguments.'

They made it to the kitchen and back but by the time Kelly was sitting back on the sofa all the colour had gone from his face and he looked as if he needed to lie down.

'Cake looks amazing,' he said but Olivia wasn't fooled. He was trying to distract her with compliments but it wasn't going to work.

She had been wondering if he was right, that she could let him sleep but now she knew there was no way. She was going to follow the doctor's orders to the letter.

'Thanks to you. I've taken a photo. I think I need a record of it and I doubt any of my friends would believe that I made it, even with help.'

'It's delicious,' Kelly said with his mouth full.

Olivia ate some and had to agree.

'We can try something else next if

you'd like?' Kelly said, sipping at his coffee.

'I'd like that. Maybe you can make a decent cook of me yet.'

'I think you've proved it to yourself already,' he said, gesturing at the cake.

'I had an excellent teacher,' Olivia said, feeling herself blush just a little.

'Actually, I think there is talent there,' Kelly said, smiling. He seemed to be enjoying her mild discomfort.

'I've made one cake. One cake against the many I have attempted to make before. I think it is way too early to say.'

'We'll just have to keep going with the lessons then.' Kelly's smile told Olivia that he was enjoying teaching her as much as she was enjoying learning.

The thought made her heart beat a little faster but she quickly pushed the sensation down.

She couldn't let things go beyond friendship. Kelly was leaving. He had a dream and it was because she cared for him that she wanted him to follow it.

'I think I'm going to give Mabel that

bath now,' Olivia said and Kelly was distracted by Mabel trying to hide behind him, giving Olivia the opportunity to leave the room before she gave her feelings away.

Disturbing Find

Olivia came back into the room with an old metal tub that Kelly had found when he was clearing the vegetable patch. Olivia had cleaned it up and now it was the perfect Mabel-size bath. She placed a towel on the floor and the bath on top before returning to the kitchen for the bucket with the warm water in it. After a couple of trips the bath was full enough.

'Right, come on, then,' Olivia said to Mabel who was still trying to hide behind Kelly. Kelly reached for her.

'Look, kiddo, let's face it, you smell really bad. It's bath time.' Kelly handed over the wriggling dog and Olivia took her and placed her gently in the bath. She reached for the dog shampoo and Mabel made a break for it, spraying water everywhere.

'What you looking at me for?' Kelly asked with a wide grin. 'I'm injured.'

And he made motions with his hands to show Olivia that she needed to do the chasing. Olivia shook her head at him but got to her feet and raced after her errant dog.

Olivia skidded across the hall just as Mabel did an about turn and ran back the way she had come. Olivia turned round and raced back after her.

'She's coming your way!' Olivia shouted as she slid across the hall floor and back into the lounge. Kelly was sitting on the sofa sipping his coffee and looking innocent.

'Which way did she go?' Olivia asked, panting slightly after the running about.

'No idea,' Kelly said.

Olivia frowned and Kelly flashed her a smile before jerking his head towards the curtains that were floor to ceiling. Olivia raised an eyebrow and Kelly shrugged. Olivia crept forward, making a grab for the small lump that wasn't exactly hidden behind the curtains.

The lump, which was Mabel, wriggled for all she was worth but this time Olivia had a good hold on her.

'Come on, Mabel! You know you'll

feel better after you have a bath.' Olivia carried the still wriggling dog back to the bath and dunked her in it. With one hand holding Mabel's collar, she reached for the shampoo and squirted a generous amount on the dog's coat before rubbing it in vigorously.

'She's glaring at me,' Kelly said. 'How did she know that I told on her?'

'She's clever like that,' Olivia said without taking her eyes off the little dog. She knew that if she lost attention for a second Mabel would make the most of it and make another grand escape. Olivia rinsed the shampoo off and gave Mabel's collar a tug.

Mabel stepped out of the tub and on to the towel, all the while refusing to look Olivia in the eye. Olivia wrapped Mabel in the towel and lifted her into her arms. She took a seat next to Kelly on the sofa and started to dry her off.

Mabel's head appeared from a gap in the towel and she reached for Kelly who held out a hand and stroked her.

'It appears I am forgiven.'

'It'll take a bit longer for me, I expect,' Olivia said, giving Mabel a kiss before handing her over to Kelly. Mabel turned around three times and then settled in Kelly's lap.

'Looks like Mabel will be keeping a close eye on you overnight, too.'

'Really, I'm fine. We could all do with some sleep,' Kelly said, scratching Mabel behind her ear.

'You sleep away, just don't be surprised when I wake you up every hour.'

'Really?' Kelly said and he looked like a school boy pleading for an extra piece of cake.

'Yes, doctor's orders. And in the morning we'll go over to the mainland so the doctor can check you out.'

When the sun finally came up Olivia felt like she had been awake for at least a year. She knew she had dropped off a couple of times but hardly slept well with her alarm going off every hour.

Every hour, as she had been instructed, she shook Kelly awake and checked that he knew where he was and that he could remember what had happened. He had barely complained and Olivia knew things would have been different if they were the other way round.

Derek had replied to her text and would be at the small jetty as soon as the tide allowed. One glance at her watch told her they had an hour to get ready.

'I'm going to get us some breakfast together. Derek will be here in fifty minutes.'

Kelly stretched and yawned and Olivia thought he had more colour than the night before. He sat up slowly and gingerly felt the back of his head.

'How is it?' she asked, blinking her eyes which felt dry and itchy from lack of sleep.

'Feels OK,' Kelly said with a shrug. Olivia leaned over him and inspected the bump on the side of his head. It didn't seem to have grown from last night but judging by the way Kelly winced she knew it was painful to touch.

'We need to eat and then get ready.'

'I'll go and take a shower,' Kelly said,

getting to his feet. Mabel was now wide awake and had clearly slept well, judging by the way she was jumping all over the place.

'Do you think that's a good idea? On your own, I mean?' Olivia knew that her words could be misinterpreted but she fought back the wave of embarrassment. It was a sensible question to ask someone who had been knocked out the day before.

'I think I can manage,' Kelly said with a smile as he walked slowly towards the lounge door. 'Unless you want to come and help?' he called as he made his way up the stairs.

Olivia shook her head, glad that Kelly couldn't see the look on her face, which was a mixture of amusement and mortification. Mabel barked and Olivia shook herself from her thoughts. They needed to get ready, she didn't want to keep Derek waiting.

'Right, quick breakfast and then we are going over to the mainland.'

Mabel cocked her head to one side.

She was not the best sailor but Olivia wasn't happy to leave her behind.

'It will be as smooth as a mill pond out there, you'll be fine,' Olivia told her but to her eyes Mabel did not look convinced.

Olivia, Kelly and Mabel made it to the jetty in time to see Derek tying up his boat.

'Sounds like you've been having an adventure,' Derek said.

'No big deal,' Kelly said. Olivia looked at Kelly and raised an eyebrow. Kelly sighed, climbed into the boat and took a seat. Olivia scooped Mabel up in one arm and Derek helped her into the boat. Once she and Mabel were settled he turned the engine over and they were soon heading towards the mainland.

'You all right to walk up to the doc's, mate?' Derek asked as they stood on the jetty looking back across to Olivia's island.

'Really, I'm fine,' Kelly said, sounding like a martyr.

'I think we'll be OK,' Olivia said,

eyeing Kelly closely.

'Just ring me when you want to get back. You've got probably six hours. But you know Ruthie and I are always happy to put you up for the night.'

'Thanks, Derek,' Olivia said before kissing the older man on the cheek. Derek nodded, looking both pleased and a little embarrassed.

'Which way?' Kelly asked as Olivia put Mabel on the ground.

'Follow me.' Olivia headed along the stone jetty towards the small seaside town centre.

Olivia sat in the doctor's waiting room. She had wanted to go in with Kelly, thinking that he might not tell her what the doctor had said, but she thought that might be pushing it a bit. Mabel was sitting at her feet, straining at her lead trying to greet every person as they came through the door.

Kelly had been a while but Olivia was trying to see that as a positive that the doctor was giving him a thorough check-up rather than that there was anything wrong. She had read all the posters on the wall at least three times and so reached for the pile of free local papers that were on a side table next to her.

It was a mildly interesting read until she got towards the end of the newspaper. The last few pages before the sport were about properties for sale.

Olivia had no thoughts of buying anywhere but she always liked to look and that was when she saw it. All she could do was stare at the advert, complete with photographs, and she knew it would be perfect. The door to the doctor's office opened and Kelly stepped out with a grin on his face.

'As predicted, I am absolutely fine.'

'You will be,' Doctor Grayson said, a woman perhaps ten years older than Olivia who she knew to be a straight talker, 'if you rest for the next few days.'

Kelly's grin slipped a bit as Olivia gave him a look.

'I'll make sure of it, thanks, Jess,' Olivia said, smiling at the doctor.

'No problem. Mr Kettering, if you'd like to come this way,' Doctor Grayson said, flashing Olivia a smile before focusing on her next patient.

'Is that the local paper?' Kelly asked as Doctor Grayson closed her door behind her.

Olivia looked down at the paper in her hands and felt like she had been caught reading Kelly's diary. She wasn't sure she trusted herself to speak and so simply nodded.

'Great. I'll take a look at it later. Fancy a coffee?' Kelly said, smiling, before leading the way out. Olivia followed him, fighting the urge to throw the paper in the bin.

She knew for sure now, what she had suspected for some time. She didn't want Kelly to leave. She didn't want Kelly to leave because she loved him.

But could she keep the perfect opportunity from him? And if she did, did that mean she didn't really love him? If you loved someone, could you put you own needs before theirs?

Secret Dream

Olivia found a seat outside the coffee shop with a good view of the marina of tiny fishing boats. Most of them were out at sea collecting lobsters and crabs for the local restaurants. Mabel was sitting at her feet, watching the world go by, and Kelly was inside waiting for their coffees to be made.

Olivia could see the local paper sticking out of her bag and once more had an overwhelming urge to throw it in the bin. She knew she was being ridiculous. For one thing, Kelly could easily go and buy one from one of the shops but still she felt her fingers itching to get rid of it.

She also knew she was being unfair and selfish. If she thought the advert was the perfect opportunity for Kelly then he probably would too. Olivia pictured his face when he spoke about his long term dream and felt a fresh wave of guilt.

She couldn't keep this from him, not if she truly cared about him. She didn't want him to leave. She wanted him to stay, so that she had more time to get to know him and to explore whether her feelings were real or just a reaction to the fact that she had a kind person in her life who seemed happy to put up with her artistic temperament, but that was selfish.

She gazed through the window of the coffee shop and could see Kelly chatting with the barista. He always seemed so at ease with other people and himself.

Olivia focused her eyes on her own reflection. Kelly was her friend, she told herself firmly, and friends didn't keep important opportunities to themselves for selfish reasons.

As Kelly came out of the coffee shop Olivia made up her mind. No games, no tricks. This was what Kelly wanted and Olivia was going to do everything in her power to get it for him. He had done so much for her, she owed him that, at the very least.

Kelly placed two mugs of coffee and a plate of bacon sandwiches on the small table, which rocked slightly.

'I thought you might be hungry,' Kelly said and Olivia's stomach rumbled as the smell of fried bacon wafted up to her nose. Mabel was paying much more attention now, too.

'And I have something for you,' Kelly said, addressing his comment to Mabel as he pulled a handful of dog biscuits from his pocket. He put them on the ground and Mabel fell upon them as if she hadn't been fed in days.

'There was something interesting in the paper,' Olivia said, knowing that if she didn't start the conversation she would chicken out.

'Oh, yes?' Kelly said, seeming more interested in the tasty food than anything in the paper.

'It's a small piece of land with some derelict buildings on it.'

Kelly looked up and had stopped chewing, Olivia knew she had his attention.

'The farm next to it is organic, like a large smallholding.'

Kelly wiped his hands on a paper napkin and held out a hand for the newspaper, which Olivia handed to him.

'Page forty-two. Seems like it could be just what you're looking for . . .'

There was a part of Olivia, quite a big part, that hoped he would look at the advert and find something fundamentally wrong with it. Perhaps the land wasn't big enough, or there were access problems or something similar but as she studied Kelly's face he looked like a man who had just been handed the keys to his dream house.

'It would be perfect,' Kelly said, continuing to study the advert.

'The organic farm could supply me with fresh meat and I could grow some vegetables. There certainly would be enough land. The buildings look like they could be easily converted into a restaurant, shop and kitchen.'

Now Kelly did look up and Olivia had to smile. His expression was a mix of joy and excitement and she was immediately glad that she had shown the advert to him.

'I can't believe you spotted this. I could have missed it and I expect it will go quickly.'

'The estate agent is in town so we could go and have a chat with them and find out a bit more, if you like. We have a couple of hours before the tides turn.'

'Do you mind?' Kelly asked but his eagerness was obvious.

'Not at all. In fact I'd love to come with you.'

Olivia sipped her coffee quickly as, although Kelly was trying hard, it was clear that he was desperate to go and speak to the agent. The seaside town was small so it only took five minutes to walk to the estate agent.

It was one of two in the town but this one dealt with more unusual and larger properties. There was a bell above the door that tinkled as Kelly pushed it open. Three people, in smart suits with red ties, all looked up as they walked in.

'I'd like to speak to someone about the farmland that's for sale,' Kelly said, unable to keep the grin from his face.

'Please take a seat.' An older man, with closely cropped greying hair, indicated the chairs. Kelly took one and Olivia took the other. She scooped Mabel up on to her lap and tried to ignore the slightly disapproving glance from the silver-haired estate agent.

Olivia sat and listened to Kelly talk. He had obviously spent a lot of time thinking and planning for this next phase of his life.

She wasn't sure why that should surprise her, since that seemed to be his approach to life. He had talked about his dream before but not in the way he was talking about it now.

Before it had seemed like any other dream, one you where you imagine how wonderful it might be but never get further than that. But Kelly had plans, real plans and Olivia felt almost as if she had been left out of part of his secret dream.

She was shaken from her thoughts as Kelly was standing up and shaking hands with the estate agent. He had a bundle of paper under one arm. Olivia got to her feet and carried Mabel out of the office.

'Well?' Olivia asked. She wanted to know what he thought and besides that, she needed to hide the fact that she had tuned out of the last half of Kelly's conversation with the agent.

'It almost sounds too good to be true,' Kelly said, running a hand through his hair.

'Well, maybe you need to go and see it,' Olivia suggested. She didn't want him to, not really. What if it was perfect and he loved it? Then he would leave and it was such a painful thought that she felt her heart contract in her chest.

Kelly laughed.

'We are going to see it. We have an appointment for one o'clock.' He gave her a look which was amused, as if he knew that she hadn't been paying attention. 'I assumed you would want to come, too?'

Olivia smiled and nodded. She wanted to support him and despite her own feelings on the subject, his enthusiasm was infectious.

'I definitely need someone sensible to cast and eye over it. You know, to tell me if they think it's a good idea or not.'

'Of course,' Olivia forced herself to say as they walked back down the street. She knew she couldn't be in a more awkward position. She wasn't the sensible person he was looking for. She was selfish, wanting to keep him near her because she liked having him around.

Worst Fears

Kelly took Olivia to lunch and Kelly chatted about his ideas for the place. Olivia was happy to sit and listen. It was lovely to see him looking so animated but it couldn't shift the coldness that sat in her stomach.

They hadn't even seen the place but Olivia had a feeling that it would be exactly right for Kelly and that he would want to seize the opportunity. Olivia managed to smile and ask questions despite herself.

Inside her, the battle raged as she fought between wanting the best for Kelly, wanting him to follow his dreams and an overwhelming desire not to lose him. She squeezed her hands tight in her lap as she made her decision.

With effort she pushed aside her own thoughts and deep feelings and made herself focus. This was about what Kelly wanted and if she truly cared that should be all that mattered.

The estate agent who would be showing them the property was the youngest in the branch, dressed in a suit that made him look like he had borrowed it from his dad and with the kind of smile that betrayed some nerves.

He drove a smart new car and was tentative and over the top at the same time which told Olivia, who was sitting in the back, holding on to Mabel, that it was likely his first car and that he hadn't been driving that long.

'It will take us about forty minutes to get there as long as we don't get stuck behind any tractors.'

Olivia wondered if that was why the youngest member of the team had drawn the short straw on taking them to the viewing.

'It's beautiful countryside,' Kelly said in response.

Olivia looked out of the window and couldn't help agreeing, but it also made her realise quite how far away from the island it was. She doubted she would get to see much of Kelly. Between her painting and him setting up his new business it seemed unlikely that they would be able to spend much time together. She forced herself to concentrate on the conversation between Kelly and William, the young agent.

'You OK?' Kelly asked.

Olivia realised that her face might be giving away her innermost thoughts and so forced herself to smile.

'I'm fine, thanks.'

Finally William took a lane on the left and drove away from the sea. The lane ran through fields which were alternately filled with cattle and sheep and others which looked planted, with what Olivia wasn't sure, but it was clearly a working farm. William took another turning and pulled the car up to a stop outside a run-down barn. They all climbed out of the car and stood and looked.

'This is the main barn?' Kelly asked, gesturing towards the ramshackle building.

'Yes, the landowner has provisional planning permission for a change of use,' William said, reading the information off his notepad.

Kelly nodded and strode off towards the barn. There wasn't exactly a door, the remnants of the barn gate was hanging off at an angle and pitted with large rusted holes in the metal.

Olivia followed Kelly inside and Mabel was busy with her nose to the ground, taking in all the smells. Olivia was hard pressed to say who was most excited between Kelly and the dog.

Olivia looked up and could see that inside, the barn was older than she had expected. There were three original brick walls which had been encased by the metal structure outside.

The brick walls were supported by aged beams of wood and if you could overlook the state of disrepair and the faint odour of animals then even Olivia could see that it had potential.

'It's an amazing space,' Kelly said, walking around and running his hand along the brick walls.

'It comes with a small amount of land

and access from the main lane. The landowner has put a few caveats on the sale as he wants to ensure that it remains in keeping with his philosophy — so no weekenders.' William glanced at Kelly and then Olivia as if he was trying to work out if they fitted into that category. 'He wants to sell to a traditional business.'

'Well, I would be looking to set up a restaurant and organic produce shop,' Kelly said, grinning at Olivia who had to grin back. Whatever her own feelings it was wonderful to see Kelly so excited.

'I would need to check with the owner that your plans would fit within his expectations,' William said, sounding a little doubtful.

'Surely that would be traditional enough for him?'

'I'm sure it would,' William said, plastering a smile on his face as if he had remembered some piece of training that told him he always had to be upbeat.

Kelly had walked out through a gap in the back wall, which Olivia was sure was not there by design. In his hand he had the land description.

'So out to that fence over there,' he said, pointing, 'and then along this line here.'

'Would that give you enough room for growing food?' Olivia asked as Mabel started to dash around the enclosed space.

'Plenty — and room for chickens. Maybe even more than that.'

'It's a beautiful spot,' Olivia said, taking a moment to take in the view. The ground behind the old barn sloped gently upwards and they walked together to the fence before turning and taking in the views of the sea in the distance.

'It's perfect,' Kelly said, his eyes moving back to the barn. Olivia knew that in his head, he was planning what it could look like and she knew that she would do whatever she could to encourage him to buy it.

He seemed so excited, had such a vision for his own future that she knew she couldn't and wouldn't try to stop him — not even if it broke her heart. She had survived that before and she would again.

'So you'll need finance in place and some provisional plans of what you want to do with the place. The landowner will want to review both and then will ask you to sign a contract with regards to what the land can be used for.

'It will become a legal clause on the property and land,' William said as he drove them back to the office.

'I understand. Can you tell me if there is any other interest?' Kelly asked as William drew up outside the estate agent's.

'There has been some interest but the landowner is keeping his options open.'

'Fair enough. I'll get my documents together and get back to you as soon as I can.'

'That would be advisable,' William said, holding out his hand which Kelly shook.

Kelly and Olivia walked back towards the harbour with Mabel trotting at their heels.

'If you can give me some idea of what you want it to look like, I can do you a watercolour? I mean I know you will need proper architectural drawings but it might help share your vision with the landowner.'

'You'd do that for me?' Kelly asked.

Olivia wanted to tell him that she would do anything for him but knew that she couldn't. Not now. Now she needed to bury those feelings deep and help him achieve his dream. Her phone beeped and she pulled it out of her pocket.

'Derek says we have about an hour or we'll need to stay overnight.'

Kelly nodded distractedly.

'Maybe you should stay,' Olivia said, swallowing down the sadness that seemed to form a band around her chest. 'It sounds like you have people you need to speak to.'

'Do you mind? After all, I still work for you.'

Olivia forced herself to smile.

'You do more than enough and besides, you haven't had a day off since you arrived. I think I owe you some time.'

'That would be amazing. I'll get it done as quickly as possible.'

'No rush. Do what you need to,' Olivia said. She knew she was going to have to get used to being on her own again so she may as well start now.

'In that case I'm going to go to my bank and see if I can get an appointment.'

'Good idea,' Olivia said, but the words were barely out of her mouth before he had turned and was heading back up the hil. Olivia looked down at Mabel.

'Just the two of us again, Mabel, but we'll be all right.'

Mabel pulled on her lead as if she wanted to follow Kelly. Olivia knew how she felt.

She scooped the dog up into her arms and walked slowly in the direction of Derek and his boat.

Disappointment

Olivia had arrived back on the island late afternoon and it felt more isolated than it ever had before. It had always felt like a good kind of isolation, like escaping from the world, but today it felt very far away from the people she cared about.

She knew that Kelly would be back the next day but also that he would one day leave and that day was coming sooner than she had ever expected.

Mabel was running ahead of her, seemingly relieved that she was no longer on the high seas. Olivia trailed her back up the path to the house and round the back to the kitchen door.

Olivia could see how hard Kelly had been working to rediscover the previous kitchen garden. She knew that at one point in the house's history the family had grown a lot of its own food.

Kelly had built wooden growing sections, slightly raised to make them easier to work and judging by the neat rows of soil and labels had already started planting.

She opened the back door, wondering if she would be able to maintain it and the house and keep painting all by herself. She knew what Abby would say once she found out that Kelly was leaving.

Abby would want to find her someone else but the problem was that Olivia couldn't imagine sharing the island with anyone else.

She sighed and threw her bag on the kitchen table. There were plenty of meals in the freezer that Kelly had made up but she couldn't quite bring herself to eat any of them. Instead she dug deep and found a ready meal, a shop brought one that had been in there for goodness only knew how long.

Throwing it in the microwave and waiting for the ping did nothing for her mood. Mabel was dancing around her feet and so Olivia poured some dog biscuits into her bowl and Mabel set about eating with gusto. Olivia remembered the sensation of tucking into Kelly's meals the same way.

She wondered if he would do some sort of take on ready meals that she could buy and fill up her freezer but in truth she wasn't sure that she could face the thought. Perhaps it would be best to go for a clean break.

When the phone rang, for a heart-beat Olivia thought it would be Kelly, perhaps checking in or telling her that he had changed his mind that the land wouldn't work for him. As she read the name on the phone she pushed that self-ish thought away, knowing it was both unfair and unkind.

'Hey, Abby,' she said, trying to sound like all was right in the world.

'What's the matter?' Abby said instantly and Olivia allowed herself a small smile at the thought she could get anything past her friend.

'Nothing,' Olivia said. 'Well actually, Kelly had a bit of an accident.'

Olivia heard Abby's sharp intake of breath and was instantly reminded of another phone call. The one when she had to tell Abby about what had happened to Ted.

'Nothing like that,' she added hurriedly and pushed the memory from her mind. 'He's fine. He slipped on some rocks going after Mabel and knocked himself out.' There was a pause.

'Are you OK?' Abby asked.

'It was Kelly that knocked his head, Abby,' Olivia said, even though she knew exactly what Abby was getting at.

'You must have been very frightened.'

'I was but Kelly came round quickly and the doctor checked him out today and said that he was fine.'

'Well,' Abby said briskly, 'it just goes to prove my point that you shouldn't live on the island on your own, doesn't it?'

'Yes, Abby. You were right as always.' Olivia paused, almost ready to tell her that Kelly was leaving but at the last moment she couldn't do it.

It wasn't as if Kelly had made any concrete decisions yet. No, better to leave it and wait and see. Maybe Kelly would change his mind.

* * *

The next morning and Olivia was determined to put on a brave face. She didn't
want to give Kelly the idea that she
couldn't cope without him.

If Kelly stayed out of some sense of
responsibility for her, she knew that
would be worse than asking him to
choose between her and his dream and
she wasn't about to do that either.

She cooked herself a proper breakfast
of scrambled eggs on toast, took Mabel
for a morning stroll and then settled
down to paint.

The only problem was that all she
could think of to paint was Kelly's barn.
Knowing that was the way her inspiration worked she gave into the desire and
by lunchtime she had completed a small
watercolour of the barn in its current
state.

She stretched out the kink in her neck
and stood up before heading into the

kitchen in search of food. On the kitchen table was a bag of shopping.

She stopped for a moment wondering if she had some sort of squatter before telling herself firmly she was being ridiculous since she doubted they normally brought food with them and left it in a stranger's kitchen.

Glancing out of the window she could see a figure bent over, working in the vegetable garden and she knew in an instant that it was Kelly.

She had no idea that he was even back and a glance at the clock on the kitchen wall told her he was much earlier than she had expected.

Judging by the way that Kelly was digging, she had a strong feeling that something had not gone well. She filled the kettle and popped it on the stove to boil before turning her attention to the bag of food.

When she had sandwiches made with the fresh bread, ham and salad and two cups of tea ready she moved over to the kitchen door and pulled it open.

'Hi,' she said, feeling a little uncertain how Kelly might react.

'Hello,' he said but Olivia could detect the forced cheerfulness in his voice.

'I've made us some lunch,' Olivia told him, feeling that Kelly might feel better once he had eaten something.

'Thanks but I'm not hungry,' Kelly said, driving the fork in to the earth and turning it over.

'Aren't you the one always telling me I need to remember to eat?' Olivia braced herself, expecting Kelly to respond crossly but instead he sighed and leaned the fork against the wall of the house.

'I suppose I am,' he said and managed a small smile.

'Come on then,' Olivia said.

They ate in silence. Olivia was desperate to find out what had happened but she knew that Kelly would tell her when he was ready.

'The veggie garden is coming on well. I didn't realise you had started planting.'

'At least one thing is,' Kelly said morosely.

'Right, I'm going to make us another cuppa and dig out the rest of the cake and then you can tell me all about it.'

Kelly shrugged and Olivia wasn't sure whether he wanted to talk about it or not.

'Whatever it is, I'm sure it's something we can work out,' she added, torn between hoping that was true and wondering whether Kelly would decide he would be happier with her on the island.

'I don't need to burden you with this,' Kelly said, cradling the mug of tea that Olivia had put in front of him.

'Hardly a burden,' Olivia pointed out and took a bite of cake to give her an excuse to stay silent and wait for Kelly to speak.

Kelly sighed.

'Let's just say the bank weren't as enthusiastic as me.'

'Oh,' Olivia said, knowing there wasn't much more she could say. She did have some money saved, working on building up enough money to do up the house and open the artists' retreat.

160

'Well, maybe I could help?' She didn't think she could bear to see the look on his face, such a transformation from the excitement the day before. 'I have savings. Perhaps I could lend it to you for a deposit?'

Kelly shook his head.

'I can't ask you to do that. You need it for this place.'

'I do, but it's not going anywhere and you've sorted out the most urgent repairs. Once you have your place up and running you can pay me back.'

'No.' Kelly sounded angry and Olivia was a little taken aback. She had thought Kelly might refuse her offer but didn't expect him to be angry with her.

'Why don't you think about it? Take some time. There's no rush.'

'I said no,' Kelly said, standing up suddenly and making Olivia jump a little. 'I'm going to get back to work.' His voice softened a little but his anger was still evident.

'I should be getting back to work, too,' Olivia said, standing up too. Kelly nodded curtly and then walked out of the back door before closing it behind him.

Mabel leaned against Olivia's leg and she leaned down and picked her up.

'What was that about?' Olivia asked the dog who reached up and licked her nose. 'Well, I think he needs some time and space.'

Mabel barked once and Olivia was convinced she understood every word.

'So you need to come and hang out in the studio with me.'

Olivia put the painting of the barn out of sight and set to work on another project, stopping only when the light started to fade. She hoped that Kelly had worked out some of his mood on the garden and that he might be more open to talk about it. At the very least she hoped the atmosphere would change. She had felt it all afternoon and it wasn't a comfortable feeling.

She pulled open the door from the studio and walked into the kitchen, half expecting to see Kelly there making supper. Instead there was a handwritten note on the kitchen table top.

'Chilli con carne in the fridge, just needs heating up and some rice cooking. Gone out for a walk. Don't wait up.'

Olivia found a bottle of red wine and opened it, pouring herself a glass. Kelly's reaction was understandable she supposed. He had obviously had trouble at the bank raising the funds for his dream and that disappointment must be hard to bear.

What didn't make sense was his angry response to her offer and that hurt. It was a side to Kelly that she hadn't seen before.

Of course she knew that everyone had moods and couldn't possibly be happy all the time, but still . . . The fact that he had now gone out of his way to avoid her seemed to compound the issue.

It was dark outside and walking in the dark could only have one motive, couldn't it? To avoid her. To avoid any kind of conversation.

For the first time in the months since

Kelly had arrived, Olivia was almost glad to be alone. And she made up her mind.

If Kelly wanted to be left alone then that was exactly what she was going to do.

Carried Away

When Olivia woke in the morning there were no sounds from the house. She figured that Kelly must have come in late and was still asleep. She slipped quietly down the stairs. She had been up late thinking and had decided that perhaps she had judged Kelly a little harshly.

She remembered with a mixture of embarrassment and pain how she had reacted when her own dreams had been crushed. It was one of the reasons that she had decided to undertake her self-imposed exile to the island. She could hardly blame Kelly for being upset and angry in a similar situation. And that's what she planned to tell him, over breakfast.

Olivia had everything ready and still there was no sign of life from Kelly. She had kept Mabel in the kitchen with her but now she opened the door.

'Where's Kelly?' she said to the small dog. 'Go find him!'

She waited at the bottom of the stairs as Mabel raced up them. Mabel disappeared out of sight and then Olivia could hear barking. She chuckled to herself at the thought that Mabel was waking up Kelly loudly but then Mabel appeared at the top of the stairs, still barking.

Olivia walked up the stairs, frowning. Was Kelly still so upset that he was refusing to get up? That didn't seem like the Kelly she knew but then she had seen a distinctly different side to him yesterday.

At the top of the stairs she turned in the direction of Kelly's room. The door stood slightly ajar, evidence that Mabel had been inside. What was strange was that Mabel never took no for an answer and would pester a person until they gave in and got out of bed.

Olivia knocked gently on the door but there was no reply. She pushed at the door and knew immediately that Kelly was not in his room. The bed was neatly made, as you would expect from someone who had been in the army.

The curtains were open and there was

little sign that the room was occupied, but then Kelly had only brought a rucksack with him so that wasn't so much of a surprise. What was a surprise was the fact that Olivia was now sure that Kelly had not been home overnight.

She could feel her heart start to hammer in her chest as she conjured images of the time they had gone out looking for Mabel and Kelly had slipped and knocked himself out.

He had been told by the doctor to take it easy. What if something had happened to him? The very thought of that made Olivia gasp in fear.

Mabel stopped running around and started to whine next to her. Olivia forced herself to take a deep breath.

She quickly formed a plan, grabbed a rucksack from her room and stuffed in an old blanket. She ran down the stairs and grabbed the first-aid kit, her mobile and some water, before clipping Mabel on to her lead.

Olivia was fairly certain that Mabel would be able to find Kelly, wherever he was. With one last check to make sure that her phone had enough charge she and Mabel set out.

Mabel tugged on the lead, clearly wanting to be able to run ahead but Olivia didn't want to lose her, too, and so kept a tight hold.

'Easy Mabel, we'll find him,' she muttered, although she knew she was trying to comfort herself as much as the dog. Mabel barked in response and tugged some more. Soon Olivia was jogging along behind her. She was wearing her deck shoes and realised she should have taken the extra two minutes and put on her walking boots which would be much more suited to the terrain of the island.

Mabel led her down the narrow path to the beach where Derek would pull up his boat but there was no sign of Kelly there.

They jogged along the beach and then headed up the dunes at the far end. At the top they were high enough to see some distance but still Olivia could find no sign of Kelly.

She turned and looked out to sea. There was no way off the island without calling Derek and she knew that Derek wouldn't sail the crossing after dark unless it was an emergency. Olivia couldn't see Kelly asking Derek to take such an unnecessary risk.

But what if he had called Derek overnight and Derek had picked him up early? Surely Kelly would have left her a note? To do otherwise was cruel, letting her worry.

Olivia dug her phone out of her pocket, wondering if she should call Derek, but decided against it. There was no point worrying him when there might be a logical explanation.

Mabel barked and suddenly tugged on her lead and Olivia's phone slipped out of her hand. Olivia reached for it but as she did Mabel tugged one last time and she lost grip of the lead. Mabel disappeared off into the distance, barking.

Olivia grabbed her phone and when she turned it over she realised the screen had cracked. But she had no time to worry about that now. She needed to follow Mabel.

She scrambled over the rocky, sandy surface, once more regretting her choice of shoes as her left foot slid off a rock and her ankle gave way, pitching her sideways so that she caught her elbow and her cheek on the rocky ground.

There was no pain for a moment and then it felt like it was flooding over her and threatened to overwhelm her completely.

She felt her cheek. There was a graze but she wasn't bleeding. Her elbow was sore but she could move it. Pushing herself up on to her knees she gingerly tested her left foot. As soon as she put any weight on it she felt a sharp stab of pain but she could cope with that; at least it would take her weight.

She looked down at her phone as she wobbled a little on the spot, wondering if now was the time to call Derek. She pressed the on button but nothing happened. Once more she told herself off firmly for rushing at things and not taking care. She was about as far away from home as she could be with no phone and a sore ankle.

Mabel's barking drew her attention and so she hobbled in the direction of the bark. She walked down a sandy bank away from the beach and could see a small camouflage tent pitched in a hollow. There was a small fire going, surrounded by a circle of stones and a tin kettle perched on top.

She shook her head at her foolishness. Of course Kelly was OK. He was a soldier and could look after himself. Why did she not think that perhaps all he needed was some space?

Part of her wanted to turn and run back to the house, to pretend that she hadn't rashly raced after him but she knew that her ankle was not about to let her do that.

A figure appeared in the distance and raised a hand. Olivia could just make out Mabel dancing around Kelly's feet. Well, at least neither of them were lost. All she had to do now was try to explain to Kelly why she was here, looking rather worse for wear.

Olivia moved slowly in the direction of the campsite, trying to hide the limp which was getting harder with each step. Her ankle felt like it was swelling and it was getting more painful.

'Are you OK?' Kelly called, obviously realising that she wasn't. He broke into a jog with Mabel racing ahead. Mabel reached her first and jumped up making Olivia wobble even more on the spot.

'What happened?' Kelly asked, not even out of breath.

'I slipped on a wet rock,' Olivia said, trying to make out it was no big deal but between the pain in her foot and the relief that Kelly was all right she felt like she was on the verge of tears. If Kelly was too nice to her she might lose control altogether. Before she could protest, Kelly had swept her up in his arms.

'You look like you've been wrestling with someone much bigger than you and you lost,' he said, carrying her with ease.

Once back at the makeshift camp he

set her down on a log that he had dragged to make a seat by the fire.

'Let me take a look,' he said, gently turning her chin so he could take a look at her cheek. Very gently he ran a thumb across her cheek. Olivia winced.

'Sorry . . . It's bruised but not broken. Are you hurt anywhere else but your ankle?'

'Banged my elbow but it's fine,' Olivia said. Kelly nodded but checked it out all the same.

'Again bruised but no serious damage. Let's take a look at that foot.'

Kelly knelt down and pulled Olivia's foot on to his lap. Carefully he loosened the laces but Olivia's foot had swollen so much now that she didn't think the shoe was ever coming off. She bit her lip to try and hide the pain.

'Better to cut the laces. Less painful,' he said, taking one look at her face. Olivia nodded gratefully. Kelly pulled an army issue knife from his back pocket and set to work on the laces. As gently as he could he pulled off the shoe. Olivia's left ankle was now twice the size of her other ankle. Her toes were swollen and bruising was starting to show around her ankle bone.

'Can you wiggle your toes?' Kelly asked. Olivia tried but wasn't having much luck and she dug her nails in the palm of her hand as a fresh wave of pain hit her.

'At the very least I think you have torn a ligament but you'll need an X-ray to be sure.'

'I'm sure it will be fine with some ice or something,' Olivia said, trying to remember her first aid training from all those years ago.

Kelly raised an eyebrow.

'You're not going to be a bad patient, are you?' There was a tug of amusement at the corner of his lips and Olivia knew that she was not going to win this argument.

'Fine. I dropped my phone and now it doesn't seem to work.'

'Not a problem — we'll go back to the house and ring Derek from there.'

Olivia looked at her foot.

'I don't think I can walk that far.'

Kelly laughed.

'As if I'd let you walk.'

'Then how . . .'

'I'll carry you. It's not that far.'

'Now who's being a bad patient? You're supposed to be taking it easy. Doctor's orders.'

'Olivia, I used to have to run twenty miles with a forty-five pound rucksack. I think I can carry you less than a mile.'

'Not after a head injury!' Olivia could feel panic rising.

'Fair enough, then, you hop if you're going to be stubborn . . .'

'I'm not stubborn, I'm just . . .' Olivia couldn't find the right words. Kelly locked eyes with her for a couple of heartbeats and then looked away.

She watched as he swiftly packed up his tent and poured water on the fire then he helped Olivia to her feet.

Before she could argue he had picked her up and thrown her over his shoulder in a fireman's lift.

'What are you doing?' she demanded.

'Safest way to carry someone over distance,' Kelly said. Although Olivia couldn't see his face she knew he was grinning.

One Step at a Time

Olivia and Kelly sat in the waiting room of the emergency department. It had been surprisingly quiet and so Olivia had seen nurse quickly and was now waiting to be called for an X-ray.

'What I don't understand is why you wore those shoes,' Kelly said, staring at the TV station that was showing a crime show. 'You never normally wear them when you take Mabel out for a walk.'

Mabel was staying with Derek's wife whilst they went to the hospital. Derek and his wife had given them both a telling off about how careless they were and suggested if they were going to carry on this way, they might want to get a doctor to come and live on the island.

Looking back, Olivia couldn't blame them, they had certainly managed to get into some scrapes over the last few months.

'When you weren't around when I woke up I was worried.'

Kelly turned to look at her. He seemed surprised and that made Olivia feel a little angry.

'You hadn't left a note or anything to explain you were going to stay away all night.' Olivia felt her cheeks colour. Did she sound like a mother telling off a truculent teenager? It didn't matter. She had started now, she might as well tell him the whole story.

'All I could think of was that something had happened to you. Maybe you slipped or your head injury was worse than we thought,' she added.

Kelly nodded slowly.

'I'm sorry. I didn't really think it through. I'm used to just taking off for some space when I need to. But you're right — I should have told you.'

Olivia shrugged. It didn't really matter now.

'And in my worry,' she knew panic was a better word but wasn't prepared to use it, 'I got everything together I might need but didn't think about my shoes.' Kelly and Olivia both looked at the one foot that was still clad in a deck shoe with its thin sole. 'And then I dropped my phone and Mabel ran off.'

'Ah, bad to worse.'

'Yep.' Olivia looked at her foot which was throbbing less after the kind nurse had given her some tablets to take.

Kelly ran a hand through his hair.

'I really messed things up, didn't I?'

'Nothing that can't be fixed,' Olivia said.

'This is what I do,' Kelly said.

Olivia looked at him, her face a question. She had no idea where he was going on about but she wanted to know what was going on in his head.

'When things get difficult I just leave.'

Olivia nodded slowly.

'My dad is always quick to point out that I run away when things get difficult. I left university after a term because I didn't feel like I fitted. I went back home but my dad just wouldn't leave it be, so I joined the army. Then I left that because I just couldn't do it any more . . .'

Olivia reached out for his hand and

gave it a squeeze.

'Making a decision to leave something that doesn't work for you isn't running away. It's making a choice.'

'I was up for promotion in the army. For the first time I think my dad was actually proud of me.'

Olivia nodded. She could only imagine what that was like as her own parents were always so supportive of her choices, except perhaps to isolate herself on the island.

She felt a flash of guilt and decided that she would ring them later and invite them for a visit.

Kelly had leaned forward with his head in his hands.

'But the stuff I saw . . .' He shook his head as if trying to shed the memory. 'I had to leave.' He looked at Olivia now and she knew that he needed her to understand. She wrapped her arms around him in a sort of side hug.

'You made the right choice, Kelly. You have to believe that. You did a world of good for others but there is no shame in needing to move on from that life.'

Kelly eased out of her embrace and looked at her.

'I think you are the first person ever to try and understand.'

'Well, I know what that feels like, too,' she said with a tentative smile. Kelly returned it just as the X-ray technician called Olivia's name. Kelly got to his feet and pushed her into the X-ray room.

* * *

'Personally, I think purple is your colour,' Kelly said.

Olivia was now in another room, having been told that she had fractured some bones in her foot and would need a plaster for at least six weeks. Kelly was looking at the rolls of fabric that would be turned into a plaster cast once they had been made wet.

'I don't really care,' Olivia said, still trying to process the idea of getting around on crutches for over a month.

'This one is just temporary,' a young

nurse said as he walked into the room. 'We need to do what we call a back slab, so plaster on the back and bandage around the front, to allow for swelling.

'When you come back to clinic next week they may let you have a walking boot instead of a plaster, depending on what the consultant says.'

The nurse smiled.

'So this one will be old-fashioned white, I'm afraid.'

'Olivia's an artist so I'm sure she can decorate it herself,' Kelly said with a grin.

'Really?' the nurse said. 'I dabble a bit but I kind of feel like I might need some direction, you know?'

He pulled an elasticated stocking up over Olivia's ankle and started to add some plaster to the back of her leg.

'Olivia can help you with that, too,' Kelly said before Olivia had time to reply. 'She lives on Ingleside island and is planning on setting up an artists' retreat.'

Olivia had been about to say that but hearing Kelly say it out loud made it seem more like a reality than the dream she had in her head.

'I've heard of that place, where the old artist used to live? Didn't he leave it to someone he had never actually met?'

'That would be me,' Olivia said with a smile. 'Apparently he liked my work,' she added.

It was always so hard to explain when she didn't really understand it herself. Some mornings, when she woke up, she would still pinch herself.

'That's amazing,' the nurse said, smoothing down the last bit of plaster. 'Right — we'll get you some crutches and I'll show you how to use them.'

'Thanks, and perhaps I could have your e-mail address? I thought maybe you would like to come over and have a go at painting on the island? You could be one of the first group.' Olivia felt a little shy at the offer, wondering if the nurse's interest had just been polite conversation that he must be well used to making.

'That would be amazing! Thank you,'

he said and his face showed that the feelings were genuine.

He disappeared for a few moments and then reappeared with a set of crutches and a piece of paper with his details written on it.

'Take it easy on these until you get used to them,' he said with a smile.

'I will and I'll you know as soon as we are open for artists.'

'Brilliant,' he said with a beaming smile. 'You've made my day.'

★ ★ ★

Olivia moved slowly and Kelly walked beside her.

'I don't think we're going to make it back across tonight.'

Olivia nodded. Secretly she was quite relieved. Now that all the adrenaline had worn off she was exhausted and all she wanted to do was lie down and put her throbbing leg on a pillow.

'But we should be good for the morning.'

'Keen to get back to your vegetable patch?' she asked, half joking.

'We need to get back so we can get ready,' Kelly said. Olivia frowned.

'Ready for what?'

'For your first painting course,' Kelly said, walking off as Olivia stood where she was, on one leg, and stared.

'Painting course?'

Kelly turned back to her.

'I assume you still want to do that?'

'Of course, but . . .'

'But what? There's no time like the present. What are you waiting for?'

Kelly was distracted by the arrival of the taxi that he had called to take them back to Derek's house. He held out his arm and the taxi drew up beside him. Olivia was still standing where she had been and staring.

What was going on? Kelly had been supportive of her plans but now he seemed to want to move them on and quickly.

Perhaps he wanted to get her set up before he left? That would make sense,

185

she thought. Although how she would run the course and provide accommodation and food to the artist guests on her own, she had no idea.

Kelly didn't mention the course again until the next day when they were back on the island. As he hadn't brought it up at Derek and Ruth's house, Olivia was starting to think she had imagined the whole conversation.

Maybe she just wanted him to stay so badly that she was putting words into his mouth.

Kelly had insisted on borrowing a wheelchair for her and was wheeling her back to the house when he broached the subject again.

'So what's the ideal number of students at one time?' he asked out of the blue but sounding as if he had was just continuing on a conversation.

'Students?' Olivia asked, gripping the arms of the wheelchair as Kelly pushed it over a particularly bumpy part of the path up to the house.

'Maybe you don't call them students?

186

Fellow artists?'

'Oh, er . . . well, I think it would depend how many we can provide accommodation for. If we had to rely on the tides and getting people back and forth that is going to cause lots of problems.'

'So the house has what — six bedrooms?'

'Two more in the main bit of the house and then the attic rooms, but they would need a lot of work to get them to a state where I could actually invite people to stay in them.' She turned her head so that she could glance up at Kelly.

'But there's a lot of things that would need to be sorted before we worry about that.'

'OK, well, let's make a list. I know that you aren't going to be able to do that much and need to keep painting, but I'm sure I can make a start.'

Olivia wanted to ask him what had happened. Why was he all of a sudden so keen to help her follow her dream? What had happened to his?

He had said that the bank wasn't keen

but that was something that could be overcome. She was sure she could help him out and if she did, that might be enough to convince the bank to help out with the rest.

She couldn't help him if she spent all her savings on the house. She doubted she even had enough to cover the work that needed doing to set up the house and the course.

The real problem was that Olivia didn't pay all that much attention to her finances, at least not since she had come to the island. At first, she just couldn't make herself care enough to be involved, and that was when Abby had stepped in.

Olivia's life had improved and it made her blush to think that she had continued to let Abby sort everything out for her as if she an invalid who was incapable of looking after herself.

No — the first order of business was to speak to Abby and see where she was at and then to take back some of the responsibility that she had dumped on her best friend.

Kelly wheeled Olivia through the front door as this had a much smaller step than the back. Once indoors, with the brakes on, Olivia got out of her chair and up on her crutches. She still hadn't exactly mastered the art but at least she could get around.

'You hungry? Thirsty?' Kelly asked.

'I'm still full from lunch,' Olivia said with a smile. Kelly had bought fresh seafood and made her, Derek and Ruth a lovely fresh seafood salad.

'Great. Well, I'm going to get back to the vegetable garden. We need to get some things growing for our future guests. I'll cook supper for eight if that suits?'

Olivia nodded, still trying to process the 'we' part of his statements. Did he mean he was planning to stay?

Yesterday it was all she wanted but now she knew that his own dream was in reach, she didn't think she could live with herself if she let him give up on it so easily.

'Great — and over supper we can start

working on that list.'

Olivia stood in the hall and watched Kelly walk away and took a deep breath. She needed to speak to Abby and then work out what she could do to help Kelly. Then all she needed to do was persuade him to let her help him.

Something told her that it wasn't going to be easy but one step at a time.

A Problem Shared

The sun was shining through the windows as Olivia sat in her studio with her mobile phone next to her ear. Mabel had found a sunny spot and was sunbathing.

'Abby? It's Olivia.'

'Livvy? How's the foot?'

'Broken and in plaster but hopefully I can have a walking boot when I go for my next appointment.'

'I'm just glad you weren't badly hurt. What were you doing out there in the wrong shoes?'

Olivia rolled her eyes, realising that Kelly had told Abby everything.

'I was worried about Kelly as he wasn't there in the morning. His bed hadn't been slept in and he hadn't left a note. I was worried something might have happened to him.'

There was a pause on the other end of the phone.

'That must have been tough for you.'

Olivia swallowed as a lump formed in

her throat. She had worked hard to keep the memories at bay but now that Abby was being so understanding she knew that they would come flooding back.

She cleared her throat.

'The important thing is that he was fine.'

'Actually, I think the important thing was that you like him enough to be worried.'

Olivia allowed herself a small smile. If Abby had said that when she had first told her what had happened then she would have been upset, thinking that Abby had forgotten what she had been through.

But now, well now it was simply acknowledging the facts and allowing Olivia to take some baby steps forward. She sighed.

'I knew it,' Abby said, somewhat triumphantly. 'I thought he was lovely when I met him. I wondered if you would come to think the same. I can't believe you didn't tell me!'

Olivia glanced at the studio door to

make sure it was firmly shut and that she couldn't be overheard.

'There wasn't anything to tell. He's nice and I like him. That's all.'

'It's OK to have feelings for someone, you know. Ted would want you to.'

Olivia nodded. She knew that Abby was right. He certainly wouldn't have wanted her to spend the rest of her life alone and sad.

'You OK?' Abby asked, and her voice was softer now.

'Yes,' Olivia managed to say as a fresh wave of emotion rose up. She took a deep breath. 'I'm fine.'

'How does Kelly feel?'

'I don't know,' Olivia said, hoping that Abby wasn't going to volunteer her services as a matchmaker.

'Well, have you told him how you feel?'

'No!' Olivia said, louder than she intended, and she looked back to the door and hoped that her shout couldn't be heard in the kitchen garden.

'It's complicated,' she added, hoping that might stop the conversation.

'Life is always complicated, Liv. But you can't let that stop you.'

'But I don't want to hurt him.'

'What makes you think that you would?'

'Because maybe it's too soon. What if I take that first step and tell him how I feel and then I can't go any further?'

There was silence at the other end for a few moments.

'Do you want to know what I think?'

Olivia thought about it.

'Yes . . .' she said tentatively. Maybe her friend could help her sort through her thoughts.

'I think it is going to be hard whether it's now or in ten years. Letting yourself love someone new is going to be admitting to yourself that Ted is really gone.'

Olivia felt tears start to collect and roll slowly down her cheeks.

'You aren't going to know unless you try and I am positive if you tell Kelly what happened he will understand.'

'How much did you tell him?' Olivia croaked in a sort of half whisper.

'Only that you have experienced a loss and that you were still healing.'

'So he might just feel sorry for me. That's not what I want.' Olivia felt panic rise inside her at the thought of it.

'Liv, even if he did, I don't think he is the sort of man to give someone false hope out of some sort of misguided sympathy vote.'

'That's not all of it,' Olivia said, deciding that she had come so far she might as well come clean with the whole story.

'I had a feeling it wasn't,' Abby said dryly.

'Kelly wants to set up his own place, where he can grow and sell his own food.'

'He told me.'

'Well, I found him the perfect place.'

'OK . . .'

Olivia sighed in frustration that her friend wasn't getting it.

'On the mainland.'

'So . . . ?'

'So he's going to live somewhere else.'

Olivia couldn't believe that she had to spell this out.

'Oh, you mean like my other half?'

Olivia stopped still. That was a good point. Abby's husband, Dan, worked away a lot but they made it work.

'OK, but he is going to be all caught up in setting up his own business. The last thing he needs right now is a fledgling romance.'

'He told you that, did he?' Abby asked in her dry tone once more.

'No,' Olivia said crossly, knowing that her friend could see through her, 'but there's more.'

'Tell me.'

'The bank weren't helpful.'

'Ah, well that would be a spanner in his dream.'

'So I offered to lend him some money.'

'Right.' There was another pause from the other end of the phone. 'And was that when he took himself off for the night?'

'Uh huh.' Olivia was feeling wrong-footed, as if Abby was putting pieces together that she had been unable to do.

'And have you talked to him about it?'

'Not since I broke my foot and since

then he was been talking about getting the house ready for the artists' courses.'

'Well, that's a good thing, isn't it?'

'Not if he's giving up his dream because he thinks I need help with mine!'

'You do need help with yours. You aren't exactly the DIY queen and that was before you broke your foot.'

'But if he stays, he'll resent me.'

'And I suppose he told you that, too?'

Olivia stuck her tongue out at the phone, despite the fact that she knew Abby couldn't see her. Abby laughed.

'Look, Liv, I love you but you have got to stop having imaginary conversations with people. Truth is neither of us knows what Kelly is thinking or feeling. You need to ask him.'

'What if I can't?'

'Well, then you will be tying yourself up in knots for a long time and you might miss your chance.'

'But it's so complicated.'

'Olivia, I honestly think that most of that is in your head. Talk to him. Find out what he is thinking and feeling.'

Olivia knew she was supposed to say something but her mind had conjured up an awkward conversation where Kelly was embarrassed by her declaration of feelings and making plans to leave as soon as possible.

'You're better off knowing how he really feels than torturing yourself with possible outcomes.'

Olivia sighed.

'Go to talk to him now and call me back.'

'He's busy in the garden.'

'Fine.' Abby let out a sigh of frustration herself. 'Talk to him over supper and a glass of wine and then text me.'

'OK.'

'Promise?'

Olivia bit her lip. She knew if she promised, Abby would hound her until she did.

'Fine, I promise.'

'I'll be on that phone if you don't let me know, so no chickening out!'

'As if I would!' Olivia said indignantly and then hung up the phone with the sound of Abby's laughter ringing in her ears.

Now all Olivia had to do was decide what she was going to say. Deep down she knew that Abby was right. Up till now she had just been guessing at Kelly's thoughts and feelings and she wouldn't find out the truth unless she actually asked him.

The problem was, she wasn't sure she wanted to hear the truth. What if he wanted to be just friends? If that was the case, she supposed it would be easier if he did buy the property and move to the mainland. That would give her time to sort out her own feelings.

Olivia spent most of the afternoon staring at a blank piece of canvas, she just couldn't think about anything other than the conversation she was going to have with Kelly.

Once she knew how he felt and what his plans were, surely she would feel better, then she would be able to concentrate and work out her own plan for moving forward. Her mind was still mulling this over when there was a soft knock at the door.

'Olivia? Supper will be ready in ten.' Kelly's voice floated through the closed door.

'OK, thanks,' she said, looking at the blank canvas once more and feeling a little guilty.

It was one thing for Kelly to make supper if she was working but she hadn't actually done anything today but moon around like a lovesick teenager.

If nothing else, she needed to talk to Kelly so she could get back to painting, so that was what she was going to do. Tell him how she felt and then take her chances with what happened next.

No Further Forward

Olivia hopped into the kitchen on her crutches and took in the delicious smell.

'I thought I'd do roast lamb. I figured we deserved it,' Kelly said as he seemed to be juggling pots and pans.

'Smells wonderful,' Olivia said, sliding into a chair and leaning her crutches against the wall.

Kelly put a jug of gravy on the table and handed Olivia a bottle of red wine.

'You pour and I'll finish dishing up.'

Olivia poured two glasses and watched as Kelly put serving dishes with roast potatoes, roast parsnips and four different vegetables on the table. Then he presented her a plate with sliced freshly roasted lamb and Olivia smiled in appreciation.

'I'm glad you're hungry. It's been quite a few days, hasn't it?'

Olivia nodded, thinking that Kelly didn't know the half of it.

'Is your foot OK?'

Olivia nodded again and scooped up a mouthful of lamb to give her a few more seconds before she knew she had to say something.

Kelly took an appreciative sip of wine.

'I wanted to talk to you, actually,' he said.

'Oh?' Olivia wondered if it was just possible that Kelly was going to confess his undying love and save her having to broach the potentially awkward subject herself.

'I owe you an apology.'

Olivia looked at him. He wasn't wrong but that wasn't what she was hoping to hear.

'You made a very kind offer and I reacted badly to it. It was incredibly kind and generous of you and I'm sorry I didn't say that at the time.'

'That's OK. I may have overstepped. You know I didn't mean to make you feel . . .' Olivia waved a hand in Kelly's direction as she wasn't exactly sure how she had made him feel.

'What I should have told you was that

my dad had agreed to be a guarantor on the loan.'

'Well, that's good, isn't it?'

'Not really, as he has vetoed the place.' Olivia frowned. 'My dad likes to control everything. He said he would help with the loan if he was happy with the purchase.'

'Oh — and he didn't like it? It seemed perfect to me.'

'Me, too, but he said it would be a poor investment. That the business would fail and he would be on the hook for the costs. The bank won't lend me the money without my dad's agreement.'

Olivia stayed quiet. There wasn't much to say to that.

'And then when you were prepared to be so generous it made me so angry with my dad but I lashed out at you and I'm sorry — you didn't deserve that.'

'It's fine. I mean, I wish you had told me that part but I do understand.'

They ate in silence for a few moments.

'The offer still stands. I've checked on my finances and I'm sure I could be your guarantor and help with a deposit.'

Kelly shook his head.

'I can't ask you to do that.'

'You didn't ask, I offered. There's a difference.'

'What about this place and setting up the artists' retreat?'

Olivia shrugged.

'I'm in no hurry.'

'I can't ask you to delay your dream so that I can try out mine.'

'It wouldn't be a delay since I didn't have a timescale.'

Kelly was studying her closely and so she looked back at him, keeping her gaze level.

'Why would you do that for me?' he asked, his voice soft.

'Because you've done so much for me.' She decided in that moment she needed to be honest and to follow Abby's advice. 'I was stuck, going nowhere, lost in my past and you walked beside me and help me see that there was still life out there, a future.' Olivia's emotions seemed to grow within her and threatened to

204

overwhelm her.

'By cooking you some meals and making sure you eat?' Kelly said gently.

'So much more than that,' Olivia said and looked up at him. Kelly tilted his head.

'More?' he asked, his voice a little husky.

'We're friends, right?' Olivia said, knowing she was putting off what she needed to say. Kelly reached across for her hand and gave it a squeeze.

'Of course.'

'Well, for me I think it might be more than that.'

When Kelly didn't say anything, Olivia was almost too afraid to look at him. She knew that she would see the answer to her silent question in his face. She closed her eyes took a breath and looked at him. In his face she saw understanding and he gave her a small smile.

'Abby told me categorically there was to be no romance,' Kelly said seriously. Olivia blinked and then Kelly's face broke into a smile.

'I don't think it was actually written into my contract, though.' His smile was softer now and his eyes seemed to be studying her. She had no idea what to say to that.

'Olivia, I know from what Abby told me that you suffered a great loss in your life,' he continued. 'I don't know the details but I do know that it is something that you carry with you.'

'You think this is some kind of rebound?' Olivia exclaimed.

'No, but I know that it can be very difficult to move on from something like that.' Kelly stroked the back of her hand. 'And I imagine that you might be worried that it is.'

Olivia looked over his shoulder and out of the window.

'And you don't want to risk your heart on a maybe?' She said the words to the window not to him. She felt his grip on her hand tighten to a squeeze.

'I'm not worried about my heart. I'm worried about yours.'

'What is that supposed to mean?' she

asked him with a frown.

'Olivia, when your heart has been broken it can be difficult to trust your emotions. It is hard to work out whether you are ready or not to try again. I understand that, I really do.'

'So where does that leave us?'

Kelly reached across the table and lifted her chin so that they could look each other in the eye.

'That leaves us taking it slowly. As slowly as you need to.'

Olivia nodded, not sure how she felt about that. 'Did you tell me now because you thought I was going to leave?'

Olivia nodded. The tears came now and she didn't bother to try and hold them back.

'Well, we have our answer then. We both need more time. My dream isn't going anywhere but yours is right here for the taking. Getting this place up and running will give us the time we need to figure out where we are at and where we want to be.'

Olivia nodded and Kelly leaned across

and kissed her on the forehead.

'Well, if we are in agreement I suggest we get started with the list of what needs doing around here.'

Kelly produced a pen and pad, pushed his finished plate out of the way and started to write.

It was only later when Olivia had gone to bed that she had the chance to really think about the conversation with Kelly. She had texted Abby and Abby had replied with a long line of happy face emojis.

The thing that struck Olivia most was at no point had Kelly told her how he felt. She ran the conversation through her mind and knew that she was right. He hadn't said he loved her or even liked her except to say that they were friends.

Her heart sank and she reached for Mabel who moved so that she could curl up in the crook of Olivia's arm.

He had been kind and sweet but was it just his way of letting her down gently? Perhaps all he wanted was to be friends? But knowing what she had been through, maybe he was worried about knocking her back when she was so fragile.

Olivia groaned quietly and Mabel nudged Olivia's face with her nose.

'It's OK, Mabel. We're going to be OK.' And for the first time since everything had happened she knew they would be.

Kelly would stay and help her get the place ready to become an artists' retreat. Then she would help him achieve his dream. Maybe not on the farmland that was for sale right now but she would help him find somewhere else that would be perfect.

Then he could leave with a clear conscience. He would know that he hadn't led her on or given her false hope. They would remain friends. Now all she needed to do was convince her heart that that would work for her, too.

Closer to the Dream

Olivia wiggled her toes, revelling in being plaster free for the first time in six weeks. Her ankle was stiff but the bones had healed well and she had been told as long as she did her exercises, she would be back to normal within a month.

That turned out to be great timing since the artists' retreat was officially opening in four short weeks.

Kelly had worked like a man possessed and all the repairs were completed. He had also fitted two additional bathrooms as well as ensuring that the vegetable garden would be ready to produce freshly picked food for the artists' meals.

Now all that was left was the decorating of the spare rooms and making beds with the freshly ordered linens.

It seemed that a day didn't go by without Derek sailing across with a boatload of boxes and parcels.

Abby had designed a website and the first retreat was already fully booked.

Olivia still couldn't quite believe how much had changed in six short weeks.

'Look at you on two feet!' Kelly said as he walked into the studio with yet another box, this one containing paints and brushes.

'More boxes?' Olivia asked as she walked over to relieve Kelly of his burden.

'A few more, yes. Exactly how much paint do you think these artists are going to get through?'

'I just wanted to make sure I have everything they need,' Olivia said and watched as Kelly walked back out to the kitchen before carrying another box into the studio.

'I think you have that covered,' Kelly said with a grin.

'Did the paint for the bedrooms arrive?'

'Yes, but I'm not convinced you're ready to be climbing ladders just yet.' Kelly looked down at Olivia's foot which looked thin and weak when compared to the other.

'I'll manage. The whole place needs a fresh coat of paint before our open day.'

'I keep telling you I can help. I'll paint the ceilings and you can do the lower half of the wall and the skirting boards.'

'I think you have enough to be getting on with and besides, now my dream is up and running isn't it time you started working on yours? That was our agreement,' Olivia pointed out as Kelly shrugged.

'I'm keeping an eye on property coming on to the market but there isn't anything new and within my price range.'

'Have you spoken to your dad again?'

Kelly sighed and sat down on the sofa.

'I don't think there's any point. He'll only help me out if it fits his criteria and since I don't want to go back to London . . .' Kelly shrugged again.

'My offer still stands.' Olivia said the words carefully. The last six weeks had been perfect, she had enjoyed having Kelly around and felt as though they had been getting to know each other better. The only bone of contention had been her offer of money.

'You've sunk all your money into this place, and besides,' Kelly pointed out, 'who is going to cook for your guests?'

Olivia took a seat beside him on the old sofa that she had thrown a cover over.

'And I've said that as much as I love having you here I can find someone else to do the cooking.'

Kelly turned to look at her.

'You're too good to me. What have I done to deserve you?'

Olivia snorted.

'I'm hardly good to you. You've been working flat out and you're not exactly on an amazing salary.'

'It's been fun and hasn't felt like work.'

Olivia smiled. She had felt the same. They had been getting up early and working into the evenings, or at least as much as she could do with one foot in plaster but it hadn't felt like work, not really.

'I can't believe how great this place looks,' she said, turning her attention to look around the studio. It was all set up for the incoming artists.

Kelly had repaired all the windows and replaced the woodwork which was rotten in places — not to mention fixing the roof.

There was now a row of six easels set up looking out to the view of the sea in the distance. Kelly had built some work benches which would hold all the supplies that had just arrived.

'It does look amazing. I think you're going to have a very long waiting list once word gets out,' Kelly said, following her gaze.

'Now the website is up and running we are starting to get bookings in quite regularly. It's going to be busy.'

'Just as long as you make time to paint, too,' Kelly said.

Olivia sighed. She hadn't made as much time as she should have to paint, but then you couldn't do everything.

'I know,' she said, looking at an unfinished painting in the corner that had remained the same for over a week. 'But you haven't done much cooking, either.'

She turned to look at him.

'I don't want all this DIY work you're doing for me to keep you from doing the thing you love.'

'Are you kidding? In a month I'll have a captive audience to test out all my new recipes on.'

'Haven't you been trying them out on me?'

'That's different,' he said, getting to his feet. 'You're biased,' he added with a grin and then held out a hand and hauled Olivia to her feet. It felt strange to be able to stand on both feet and she wobbled a little. Kelly held on to her hand until she was steady.

'Yep, no ladders for you.'

'But don't you have other things you need to be getting on with?' Olivia protested one last time.

'Nope,' he said, striding out of the room. 'You unpack those boxes and I'll fix us some lunch. Then we can get started on that first bedroom. That awful wallpaper isn't going to strip itself.'

Olivia grabbed the first box and ran a

craft knife along the tape to open it. She had had a lot of time to think over the last six weeks but still felt nothing was clear in her mind.

She loved Kelly, she knew that. The problem was she was none the wiser as to his feelings beyond a warm friendship and he had seemed happy to keep it that way.

All her thoughts turned to the same question. Was she ready to try again?

She reached into the box and started to pull out tubes of oil paint and a tray that would hold them, before arranging them on one of Kelly's handmade tables.

She couldn't imagine this place without Kelly in it but was that just because she enjoyed his company and that he seemed to understand what she had been through. Was it just easy? Comfortable?

Those words seemed to describe friendship rather than anything more. Was that how he felt? And was he just patiently waiting until she reached the same conclusion?

He had shown no signs of wanting to

leave the island and had put his heart and soul into restoring the place to its former glory but Olivia got the impression that was the sort of person he was. When he tackled a project he did the best job he could.

'Lunch is ready!' Kelly's voice floated into the room from the kitchen.

Was it time to raise the subject again? Olivia shook her head. Until she could answer the question of whether she was ready or not she couldn't risk it.

She didn't want to hurt Kelly or make him feel somehow beholden to her. Like he was responsible for her being happy and it didn't matter how he felt.

No, she had to be sure and besides, there was another month to go. A month where they would be spending almost all their time together. She should give herself that time.

'I'm coming,' she called and tried to push all thoughts of romance from her mind.

An Unexpected Announcement

Olivia had washed and ironed all the new duvet sets and so all she needed to do now was make all the beds. It was a warm mid-summer evening and she had thought about leaving it till the morning. The problem was that the morning was the big day — the day that the first set of artists would be arriving. Better to do it now and have one less thing to do in the morning.

Olivia walked into the first guest room which she had painted a pale yellow and took in the double bed, the pretty yellow striped curtains and neat old-fashioned wardrobe.

It really was beyond what she had imagined possible for the place and she couldn't wait for others to see it, particularly Abby, who had been a firm supporter albeit at a distance.

Olivia shook out the duvet cover on to the bed and then grabbed the duvet.

With practised ease she found the corners of the cover and turned it inside out. She laid the duvet cover on the bed and turned to pick up a pillow to cover with a case. When she was finished she turned back to making the bed up.

It was then she realised there was a lump in one corner of the duvet.

'Mabel! How did you get in there?' Olivia lifted up the duvet and could see her dog curled up in one corner. 'You can't stay there. Come on.'

Mabel opened one eye but continued to feign sleep.

'I'm not falling for it. Come on,' Olivia said, trying to keep a giggle from her lips. If she started laughing then Mabel would assume that Olivia was joining her in her game and there was no hope of getting her out of the duvet any time soon.

'Don't make me come in there,' she said in what she hoped sounded like a stern voice. Mabel's tail started to wag and she knew that the small dog had not been fooled.

'Fine. I'm coming in to get you,'

Olivia said wiggling into the open end of the duvet cover and crawling towards her dog. Mabel may have looked like she was sleeping but as soon as Olivia got within arm's reach Mabel made a run for it, over Olivia's back and out of the duvet cover.

'What are you doing?' Kelly's voice sounded nearby. Olivia tried to stand up but got tangled in the duvet cover and ended up in a heap on the floor. Her landing was softened by the duvet itself which hit the floor first.

'Whoa, careful. You don't want to break any more bones.'

Olivia could feel herself blush with embarrassment and fought to find her way out. The problem was the harder she fought the more tangled she got.

'Stay still!' Kelly said, managing to squeeze the words out between gales of laughter.

Olivia did as she was told and all of a sudden she was back out in the daylight, her hair all messed up and feeling rather hot and bothered.

'If you needed help with the covers you only had to ask,' Kelly said, wheezing with laughter.

'It's all Mabel's fault,' Olivia said as Mabel sat beside Kelly looking the very image of innocence.

'Olivia, I've known you long enough to know that you are perfectly capable of getting yourself in to mischief all by yourself. There's no reason to blame your poor innocent dog.' Kelly scratched Mabel behind the ears and winked at Olivia.

'Supper will be ready soon so how about I help you finish off up here?'

Olivia nodded as her stomach rumbled.

Kelly worked efficiently, as you would expect of an army man, and between them they had rooms ready for their guests in less than twenty minutes.

They walked down the stairs together.

'I can't believe it's actually tomorrow.'

'You better believe it,' Kelly said, grinning at her as they walked into the kitchen. 'I thought a simple chicken salad was in order since it's been so hot.'

Olivia knew that Kelly didn't do anything simply and knew it would be delicious.

'Do you want to review the menu for tomorrow?' Kelly asked, taking the salads out of the fridge.

Olivia laughed.

'I've done that about a hundred times already. Your food will be amazing — as always.'

Kelly collected the freshly made salad dressing and put it on the table.

'Are you nervous?' he asked.

Olivia nodded.

'Excited, too. Are you?' She wondered if that was the reason why he had gone over and over his plans for food for the following day.

Kelly shrugged.

'Just want it all to go perfectly for you.'

'I couldn't have done half of this without you,' Olivia said, looking at him as he tucked into his salad. He glanced up at her and smiled and in that moment she knew.

She had known that she had loved him for a while but now she knew that she was ready to try out love again. Her feelings were true. Her heart leapt as she looked at him and she knew she couldn't risk him leaving without knowing how she felt.

She would never hurt him, she would never declare her love and then back away. What she needed to know now was how he felt, how he really felt.

'So I have something I want to talk to you about,' Olivia said, her words coming out as a bit of a jumble. Kelly looked up.

'Funny, so do I.'

'You first,' Olivia said, hoping that Kelly was going to save her from having to find the words herself.

'Sure?' Kelly said, and she could feel him studying her.

'Of course.'

'Well, I didn't want to say anything until I knew that I could get an agreement from the bank . . .'

Olivia's eyes went wide. She had

wondered, of course she had. After all, she had told him to keep looking for the perfect place to set up his business, to follow his dream. Now that all the work was done on the island, there was no reason for him not to.

'Go on . . .' she said, trying to infuse her voice with enthusiasm that she didn't necessarily feel. She told herself off. She should be excited for him and she was — it was just that she was battling with her own sense of loss. If only she had been ready earlier.

'It's smaller than the other place but that comes with a price tag that I can afford, at least with a bank loan.'

'That's amazing. Do you have details and photos?' Olivia asked, wondering when Kelly had had the time to go and see the place. She couldn't remember a time when he hadn't been working on the house.

'I do. Hang on and I'll show you. I haven't seen it in person yet but the photos give a feeling of the place and its potential.'

Kelly got up from the table and opened a drawer in the kitchen before pulling out some sheets of paper and handing them to Olivia.

Olivia focused all her attention on the paperwork. It gave her a few precious minutes to calm herself. She had always known that this was a possibility and she was happy for him.

He had helped her bring her dream to life in a way and at a speed that she had never imagined and now it was her turn to return the favour. That was what friends did, after all.

'The barn is smaller but the land is a bit bigger and is being sold without any kind of caveats,' he explained, 'so I can pretty much do what I like — assuming I can get planning permission.'

Olivia nodded and kept reading. She could see his vision and knew what Kelly meant about the feeling of the place. Even just from the photos she could tell that it was a special place.

'Where is it?'

'That's the only downside. It's in

Devon. About fifty miles away.'

Olivia nodded and tried to hold in her disappointment. If it had been the other place then there was a chance they would still get to see each other but fifty miles? That wasn't the kind of distance that you could meet up for dinner, not if one of you lived on an island.

'I have been looking for something closer but there really isn't anything, at least not within my budget.'

Olivia nodded again.

'It looks perfect. I can see why you fell in love with it.'

'Don't worry, I won't be leaving you in the lurch. It will take at least three months for all the legal stuff and so in the meantime I can find you the right person to take on the cooking for the courses.'

Olivia knew that his eyes were fixed on her face, trying, no doubt, to figure out what she was feeling and so she forced a smile on to her face.

'Thank you. I'd really appreciate that. Now I think we should break into some of the champagne we have for tomorrow, since we both can celebrate our dreams coming true.'

'Didn't you have something you wanted to talk to me about?' Kelly asked.

'I just wanted to thank you for all your hard work and to say that if there's anything I can do to help you achieve your dream all you need to do is ask.'

Olivia got to her feet and headed to the fridge, gulping down a swell of emotion that she was worried would overwhelm her.

What she didn't see was the look on Kelly's face as she walked away. A look which would have given her pause, made her wonder if there was more going on than she realised. But when she turned back with a chilled bottle in her hand, the look was gone and replaced with a smile.

The Big Day Dawns

Olivia hadn't been able to sleep. There were too many things on her mind. Of course it was the big day tomorrow, her dream of opening the island up as an artists' retreat was coming true and there was a lot to do. But she knew that wasn't the real reason that she had been tossing and turning all night.

She replayed her conversation with Kelly over and over in her head and the only conclusion that she could draw was that in Kelly's mind they would only ever be friends.

If that was how he felt then Olivia needed to get used to the idea. If his predictions were right then he would be around for at least another three months and so she was going to have to work hard to keep her feelings to herself.

The last thing she wanted to do was to make him feel guilty for leaving or worse, guilty that he didn't feel the same for her as she did for him. The key, she decided, was focusing on helping him achieve his dream and to keep busy.

Keeping busy was definitely not going to be a problem since the website told her the night before that even more people had booked, some for future courses and some for the artists' retreat.

At six, Olivia decided to give up and get on with the day. Abby was coming over on the first trip and it would be great to see her friend after such a long time. The day would be busy but hopefully she would be able find some time to sit down with her and have a catch up.

* * *

Olivia's wish didn't come true until well into the evening. The day had been a roaring success. She had been reunited with her parents for the first time in months and they had been both surprised and delighted by all that she had achieved. And no doubt relieved to see that she was doing so much better.

Abby had arranged for a reporter from

the main magazine for artists to attend and the young man had seemed very taken with the place and its history. All the guests who weren't staying, including her parents, had now been ferried back to the mainland by Derek and one of his friends who also owned a boat.

The six artists who were staying were sitting on benches in the garden, drinking coffee and swapping stories, with Kelly ensuring that they had everything they needed.

Once Olivia was certain everyone was settled she went in search of Abby and found her on the path to the beach talking on her phone.

'Got to go. Liv is finally free to speak to her oldest friend.' There was a pause. 'I will and I love you, too.'

Abby held open her arms and Olivia found herself well and truly hugged.

'Dan sends his love.'

'I can't believe how well it has gone,' Olivia said as her friend released her and took a step back.

'Well, I can't believe how much work

you have done. This place looks incredible.'

'Kelly did a lot of it, as I wasn't much help with one foot in plaster.'

'I was hoping you would bring him up. He looks as lovely as ever.'

Olivia smiled but she knew she hadn't succeeded in keeping the pain from her face.

'Ah . . .' Abby said. 'Want to tell me?'

Olivia nodded and sniffed.

'He has found a place. The perfect place to set up his business.'

'That's good, isn't it?'

'Its fifty miles away.'

'Well, like I've told you before, it is possible to make it work over a distance, look at me and mine.' Abby smiled kindly but Olivia was shaking her head.

'Don't you see? It's his way of telling me that he just wants to be friends.'

Abby stared at her friend.

'And how do you work that out?'

'We agreed to give ourselves time and well that time is up and he is going to be moving away.'

'Right,' Abby said in tone which suggested she had no idea where Olivia was going with what she was saying.

'It's his way of letting me down gently. If he leaves we never have to have that conversation. I know he cares and I don't think he would want to hurt me by rejecting me. This is his way of doing it without actually having to say the words.'

'And he told you this, did he?'

'No, of course not,' Olivia said crossly.

Abby sighed and crossed her arms.

'Olivia, when are you going to learn that the only way to know how someone actually feels is to ask them?'

'Don't!' Olivia said firmly.

'Don't what?' Abby asked, clearly bemused.

'Don't give me false hope. He's made his decision and I need to move on.'

'Fine, but you could be missing out an opportunity to be happy, really happy again.' Abby grinned at the mystified expression on her friend's face. 'Has it ever occurred to you that he is trying not to put you under any pressure? That maybe he has feelings, too, but he is being careful? He wants you to be sure before he says anything?'

Olivia was shaking her head and Abby reached out and caught both of her hands.

'If he thinks you aren't ready he isn't going to add to those feelings by telling you his own. Olivia, this may be one of those times when you need to make the first move.'

'But what if I do and he doesn't feel that same?'

'Then you'll be right where you are now but at least you'll know for sure.'

'But what about the barn?'

Abby shrugged.

'Maybe he thinks you can make it work over a distance? Maybe he is just planning for an alternative future if you don't tell him you love him and ask how he feels?'

Olivia thought about this. Abby always seems to make sense of things in a way that she was never able to do. None of these things had even occurred to her as a possibility.

'What I do know is that you will never find out unless you actually ask him straight out. The sooner the better.'

Olivia nodded slowly. She didn't relish the thought of asking, what if he didn't want to be with her? But Abby was right, if she did ask and the answer was negative then she would be exactly where she was right now so it couldn't really be any worse.

'Let's go back to the house. It's getting chilly.' Abby took Olivia's arm in hers and together they started to make their way along the path to the house.

They walked on for a while and then a shadowy figure appeared around the side of the house.

'There you are!' Kelly's voice sounded. 'I was beginning to think you might have deserted me and decided to head back to the mainland.'

'No chance of that, Olivia needs to be up bright and early to start teaching art,' Abby said with a smile. Then she yawned, not a particularly convincing yawn and Olivia, for one, knew that she was faking it.

'It's been quite a day. I'm going to go to bed unless you two need help clearing up?' Abby's expression was all innocence but Olivia knew that she was giving her no choice but to speak to Kelly.

'I can manage,' Kelly said. 'Why don't you both hit the hay?'

'I'll help,' Olivia said, catching a smug look on Abby's face. 'There are a few details for tomorrow that we could do with going over,' she added pointedly. Abby winked at her. All Olivia could do was hope that Kelly hadn't noticed.

'Night, then,' Abby said and hurried off into the house.

'Well, I think we can call the first day a success,' Kelly said, smiling.

'I hope so,' Olivia said her mind on what she wanted to talk to him about rather than the first day of her dream coming to life.

'You don't think so?' Kelly said, his face looked concerned.

'Sorry, I was thinking about something else. I thought the day went brilliantly, thank you for all your hard work.'

Kelly nodded thoughtfully.

'What were you thinking about?' he asked.

'Actually, there is something I wanted to talk to you about,' Olivia said, feeling as though all the air was being squeezed out of her lungs.

'Sounds serious. I'll make us some fresh coffee,' Kelly said before heading into the house. Olivia watched him go and knew needed to tell him how she felt and all she could do was hope that he felt the same.

Now or Never

Olivia sat in one of the deck chairs that they had laid out for the guests and shivered. Kelly handed her one of the blankets and then a mug of something hot.

'I went for hot chocolate instead,' he said, smiling. 'I'm not sure that more caffeine would help us sleep.'

Olivia smiled and nodded to show that she agreed as she tried to work out how to say what she felt.

'Well, I was wondering if you had given any thought to our conversation.' Olivia groaned inwardly, she was never going to find out what his feelings were unless she asked him outright and this was not the way to go about it.

'Olivia,' Kelly said with a chuckle, 'you'll have to be more specific. You and I have had a lot of conversations. Is it about tomorrow?'

'No.'

Kelly raised an eyebrow.

'Do I get a clue?'

'No, I mean . . .' Olivia sighed. Why was this so hard? 'I've been thinking a lot over the last six weeks and it's been a lot of fun getting this place set up.'

'It has,' Kelly said. He was either clueless or going to make her spell it out. The slight pinch of anger made her feel bold.

'OK. I'm going to say something and I need you not to interrupt me.'

Kelly looked at her as if to say that he hadn't been interrupting her but when he caught sight of her expression he nodded.

'You said we needed more time and I agreed but we haven't spoken about it since and in fact you never really said how you feel. Which was kind of confusing . . .' Olivia knew she was rambling but Kelly seemed to have given her his full attention.

'Anyway, Abby thinks you might not be saying how you feel because you know what I've been through and then I did tell you I wasn't sure I was ready for anything.

'The thing is, now I think I am ready but I don't know how you feel.

'And I'm worried that you might feel you can't tell me the truth after everything that happened to me but I need you to know that . . .' She paused for breath and opened her mouth to speak but then she felt Kelly's lips on hers and she lost herself in their first kiss.

They broke apart and Kelly chuckled.

'It's very complicated in your head,' he observed and Olivia smiled. He wasn't wrong.

'So let me make it simple for you. Olivia, I love you. I have from the moment I set eyes on you. And yes, Abby is right. I could tell, even without what Abby told me, that you were hurting, still grieving and I didn't want to make you feel rushed.

'I've been waiting for you to tell me how you felt and to be honest I was beginning to worry.'

'But you're buying a place so far away,' Olivia blurted out.

'Because I knew that I couldn't just

stay here and be your friend. I wanted more and I thought if you didn't then I needed to move on.'

'But I can't ask you to give up on your dream,' Olivia protested.

'Tell me what my dream is,' Kelly said and Olivia frowned. Kelly motioned that she should continue.

'You want to grow and cook your own food, in your own place.'

Kelly smiled but Olivia shook her head as if to say she didn't understand.

'Olivia, look around you. Look at what you've built. This could be my dream, if you'll have me.'

Olivia didn't know what to say. She couldn't imagine how life could come together so perfectly and so she threw herself into Kelly's arm's and kissed him.

'Is that a yes?'

'I can't think of anything I want more. I've wanted to ask you to stay but I was so scared that you wouldn't feel the same.'

'I don't think you need to worry about that any more.' Kelly leaned down and kissed her on the top of her head. 'And

I know after your experiences that we need to take it slowly.'

Olivia shifted so that she could see his face.

'What if that's not what I want?' Kelly looked surprised and uncertain at her words. 'When I lost Ted, I thought my life was over and then I met you. Ted and I were waiting to get married, until the time was right, our careers.' Olivia waved her hand to show how unimportant all of that was.

'The one thing his loss has taught me is that if you find someone to love then you grab them with both hands and you don't let go, you don't wait.'

Olivia was a little breathless after her speech but she couldn't say any more as Kelly was kissing her once more. When she pulled away, she wasn't the only one who was a little breathless.

'I've been searching for something my whole life, Liv, and now I've found it I'm not going to let it go, either. I don't need time.

I know how I feel and now that I know

you feel that way, too . . .'

Olivia giggled; she couldn't help it. She had never thought she would find peace again let alone happiness. Right now she felt so happy she thought she would burst.

'Are you sure?' Kelly said and he was serious. Olivia composed herself and nodded solemnly.

'In that case I'm afraid I'm going to have to ask you to stand up.'

Olivia stood up uncertainly. Why was Kelly so serious all of a sudden? Had he had a change of heart?

When he walked into the kitchen and away from her she thought she would burst into tears. But before she could he was back. Kelly reached for her hand and then dropped to one knee.

'Olivia, will you marry me?' he said, his voice shaking a little. Olivia's eyes went wide but she managed to process enough to make her head nod.

Kelly pulled something from his pocket and reached for her left hand. Olivia looked down as he pushed a ring of pasta on to her ring finger. She held her hand out to admire her new ring as if it were 18 carat diamonds.

'Naturally I will get you something better,' Kelly said. Olivia smiled at him.

Epilogue

of paste on to her ring finger. She held her hand out ... ... her new ring as if it were 13 carat diamonds.

'Well, Mrs Miller, don't you think this was the perfect spot for our wedding?' Kelly asked his bride as he smiled at her. Olivia looked out from his arms to the beach, where their family and friends were sitting on white chairs in beautiful sunshine.

'It's perfect,' she said, kissing him on the cheek, as Mabel, complete with a short veil flowing from her collar, barked. Kelly bent down and picked up the small dog and they shared their first official family hug.

'Our island,' Olivia said as she turned to look back at the house that had been hosting extremely successful art retreats and cookery classes for several months.

'Our island,' Kelly murmured back. 'I love you.'

'I love you, too,' Olivia said, grinning.

Together they turned to face their guests. Almost as one their friends and family got to their feet and cheered as the vicar introduced Mr and Mrs Miller for the first time. Mabel wriggled in Kelly's arms and so he set her back down on to the beach and Mabel led them back down the makeshift aisle as they were showered with rice and well wishes.

They walked together, hand in hand, to the small marquee that had been set up behind the vegetable garden, to celebrate their wedding with their friends and family and begin their new life together.